Puzzle pieces were scattered on the cement floor. Someone had hung a pink sheet up, giving the space some color. Everyone said they'd kept her locked up, isolated for years. Was this where they had put her after the accident?

Elissa started into the room, studying the stuffed animals that were gathered in the corner. The puzzle looked like it was for a young girl— a unicorn was visible on one of the stray pieces. Elissa stooped down to pick it up, when she noticed the wire bolted to one leg of the twin bed. It was pulled taut. She turned, glancing over her shoulder. All she saw was a blur as the girl charged toward her and let out a horrible scream....

FOR ERIN

Copyright © 2012 HATES
Artwork copyright © 2012 Relativity Media

Poppy

Hachette Book Group
237 Park Avenue, New York, NY 10017
For more of your favorite series and novels,
visit our website at www.pickapoppy.com

Poppy is an imprint of Little, Brown and Company.
The Poppy name and logo are trademarks of Hachette Book Group, Inc.

The publisher is not responsible for websites (or their content)
that are not owned by the publisher.

First Edition: August 2012

ISBN 978-0-316-23063-6

10 9 8 7 6 5 4 3 2 1

RRD-C

Printed in the United States of America

HOUSE AT THE END OF THE STREET

A NOVEL BY
LILY BLAKE

BASED ON THE SCREENPLAY BY
DAVID LOUCKA

FROM A STORY BY
JONATHAN MOSTOW

poppy

LITTLE, BROWN AND COMPANY
NEW YORK   BOSTON

PROLOGUE

The house at the end of Sycamore Lane was a split-level with a half-moon window in the front, its thin gray curtain always drawn. The weeds had grown up around the porch, the grass sprouting through the warped floorboards. Its shingles were splintering. Long strips of faded green paint peeled away from the frame. A rusted playground set stood in the backyard. The slide was still there, along with the metal frame, but all that was left of the swings were two broken chains. The seats had fallen off long ago, the rubber breaking apart in the sun.

It was not always this way. Things change in moments, each piled on top of the next. The family that lived in this house was chased by unhappiness, the tragic moments coming faster than the joyful ones. The fall of their

3

youngest child and only daughter, Carrie Anne, from the swing in the backyard interrupted their lives. The blood pooled beneath her head, congealing in the nest of her long blond hair. The neighbors learned the poor thing suffered brain damage in the fall, and most of her time afterward was spent indoors. She was constantly monitored by her parents. They policed what Carrie Anne ate, what she wore, and never let her out of her bedroom for more than a few hours a day. There were rumors that she was dangerous.

Years passed before another tragic moment. It was a muggy August night when it happened, a decade after Carrie Anne's accident. Her parents slept with the windows open, the air still damp from an afternoon rain shower. Mary Jacobsen, Carrie Anne's mother, awoke to the sound of footsteps in the hall. It took her a while to decipher whether it was real, or if it was part of a dream. She watched the light flicker by the crack beneath the door. John Jacobsen rolled over, noticing his wife was awake.

"How is she up again?" John asked.

Mary rubbed her eyes. "Okay, okay. I'll go," she said, an edge in her voice. They barely talked anymore. Their marriage had collapsed after the accident, with everything— every conversation, every day, every month—revolving around the girl. What would Carrie Anne eat today? Who would stay home with her while the other went into town? Unable to focus on anything except their daughter, they'd both lost their jobs in the preceding months. If they had been outside when she fell, could they have prevented it? Why hadn't John put sand on the ground underneath the swings, as he had originally promised? How many times had Mary asked him to do that?

She was always the one to console Carrie Anne when she awoke in the middle of the night. The girl needed constant comfort and guidance. Though Mary couldn't say it aloud, she'd become more callous toward her daughter. Her nerves were frayed. She scolded the girl more than she liked. In the past months she'd found herself taking too many of the pills prescribed by her doctor. She'd started seeing other physicians, desperate to get more—the supply was never enough. She and John fought most when the bottles were nearly empty.

Mary stood and walked toward the door. Her head hurt from the combination of sedatives and antianxiety medicine. When she stepped into the hallway, Carrie Anne was standing there at the edge of the stairs, her hands clasped behind her back. Mary closed the door tight behind her, knowing John would complain if they made any more noise than they already had.

"Carrie Anne," she said sternly. "You have to go back to bed."

The girl's long blond hair was tangled. It fell over her forehead, hiding her face in shadow. Her nightgown came down to just above her ankles, a dried stain on the front of it. She had lashed out during dinner, sending her plate flying across the table. Gravy had spilled over her lap. Mary simply had not had the patience to clean it up or change her clothes again.

"Carrie Anne?" Mary asked again. The girl was hunched over. She didn't respond. Mary took a step toward her, starting down the narrow hall. She hated when the girl did this—she could recognize Mary's voice. She knew she was speaking to her. Why wouldn't she just listen?

Mary took another step, reaching out her arm. She grabbed Carrie Anne's wrist, harder than she intended, and then she saw it out of the corner of her eye. Carrie Anne raised her other hand, the hammer visible in the dim hallway light. For a brief second her blue eyes shone in the dim light as she looked her mother full in the face. Then the blunt end of the hammer came down just above Mary's eye, again and again. Mary Jacobsen fell back, her face unrecognizable.

In the bedroom, John sat up, sensing something was wrong. He could hear the muffled whimpers, then the silence that followed. He was edgy from the drugs, a strange cocktail that kept him relaxed for several hours before causing rebound paranoia. He watched the door, wondering if he was imagining it. He felt for the bottle on the nightstand, but there were no more pills left.

He waited, pushing back on the bed. He watched the shadows move beneath the door, wondering if Mary had managed to get Carrie Anne back to sleep. Sometimes she had to hold the girl close to her chest, wrapping both arms around her for several minutes to subdue her. Sometimes they had to lock her into her room, listening to the screaming until it subsided. The screaming was what he hated most. He couldn't take it, the constant shrill cries, or the way the girl pounded her fists and kicked the door.

He watched the shadows move over the floor. Outside, thunder cracked. The rain started again, drenching the curtains. He squinted into the darkness, about to call out, when the door swung open. The girl rushed in, her hair in front of her face, the bloody hammer in her hand.

CHAPTER

1

FOUR YEARS LATER...

Elissa sat on the dusty hood of the beat-up SUV, her guitar settled into her lap. She leaned forward, strumming a G chord over and over again. That one had always been her favorite. Maybe it was the warm, open sound of it, or the way her fingers felt on those specific strings. Or maybe it was because it was the first chord she'd been taught. Her father had given her the guitar four years ago, when she was thirteen, as a birthday present. That was when they lived outside Chicago. That was before the divorce and all the vicious fighting that came after.

The summer that her father stopped calling, stopped coming by or writing, she couldn't put the guitar down. She'd filled the silence with music, the only thing loud enough to drown out her own thoughts. Now she eyed

Sarah, who was lying back on the hood, her head resting at the bottom of the windshield. Since her father left it had felt silly to call her "Mom" or "Mother" anymore. In his absence they felt more like roommates, moving around the shared apartment like strangers. They barely spoke to each other except to discuss household chores—who would take out the trash, who would pick up the groceries, who would wash the last dishes in the sink. It had been like that for nearly three years, until her mother announced that she'd found a house online, in a "nice" suburb of Seattle. She said it would be better for them, that they could use the time together—this fresh start—before Elissa went off to college. Elissa wanted to believe it, that being somewhere new would somehow be able to change them. But she couldn't stop thinking about something her grandmother used to say. It had been following her on the two-day road trip, trailing them across so many states. *Wherever you go, there you are.* How could a new town, a new house, make anything different? Wasn't it too late for that?

Elissa switched chords, playing the refrain of an old song by Bleeker Street. Her father had given her the album at ten, as part of her "music education." As she played she glanced over the high wall of hedges. She could just see the top of the stone house. "You must be the Cassidys!" a voice called out. She turned, looking down the road. A black luxury sedan pulled up alongside them and a short, balding man got out. "Dan Gifford. So sorry I'm late. I left my cell at the office. I'm sure you tried to call." He wiped the sweat from his forehead as he spoke.

"Only about a dozen times," Sarah said, sitting up. Her wavy blond hair fell just past her shoulders, her skin pink from the hour and a half they'd spent waiting in the sun.

"Sorry about that," Dan mumbled. "Let me show you your new home." He fumbled with a set of keys, looking for the right one. Then he unlocked the wooden gate and pushed it open, revealing the two-story stone house beyond it.

Elissa nearly laughed at the sight of it. It was ten times the size of their apartment in Chicago. The front wall had three large windows, and ornate beige pillars framed the entranceway. It wasn't enormous, it definitely wasn't a mansion, but it would still be the biggest house she'd ever lived in. She was starting to think maybe Sarah was right—maybe this would be the year things changed.

They popped open the back of the car, and Dan helped them with a few small boxes, his sweat dripping all over them. "How was the drive?" he asked, as they started up the front steps.

"We've been on the road for two days," Sarah said, leaning a box on her hip. "We're anxious to get settled."

Elissa raised her arms to grab a box of kitchen stuff and caught a sudden whiff of B.O. "And have a shower," she laughed.

Dan started up the stone steps, which were lined by

hydrangea bushes. "I think you're going to be very comfortable here. And you'll love the neighborhood."

They pushed into the foyer. Elissa couldn't help but smile. When she was a kid, she used to draw elaborate pictures of her "dream house," a two-story palace with wood floors, huge TVs, leather couches, and enough bedrooms for four kids. (She'd always imagined her parents would have more kids, when they finally stopped fighting.) This was similar. It had granite countertops in the kitchen, simple but elegant furniture, and a large deck out back. Sarah turned around, raising her eyebrows as if to say, *See?! I told you so!*

They set the boxes on the kitchen counter and started through the house, Dan showing them the three bedrooms upstairs, all furnished with queen-size beds—a luxury compared to the twin mattress Elissa had grown up with. He talked about good water pressure, some details of the rental lease, and pointed out the state park just beyond the back property line. When they were done with the tour, he pulled the keys from his key chain and pressed them into Sarah's hand. "Tomorrow the Reynoldses a few houses down are having a spring fling party. You should bring a dish and come over."

Sarah hadn't stopped smiling since they'd walked through the door. She was a terrible cook, but she nodded, as if baking some casserole was her ideal first-night-in-the-new-place activity. "We'll give you a call if anything comes

14

up," she said, her eyes on Dan as he shut the door behind him.

Elissa looked around, taking in the sliding glass doors, the curtains that were perfectly pleated, the throw pillows arranged neatly on the couch. "This is weird," she said, half laughing. "It's like a real house."

Sarah leaned in, pointing the keys at Elissa. "It *is* a real house," she corrected.

"But where are all the other houses?" Elissa asked. "Where's the bodega? Where am I gonna score my forty?" she joked, knowing her mother hated when she made any reference to underage drinking.

"That's all state park," Sarah said, gesturing out the back windows and ignoring the remark. "Pretty good backyard, huh?"

Elissa's eyes fell on the run-down estate nearly thirty yards off. It was settled into the trees, at the edge of the park's border. "Hey, we can see Mr. and Mrs. Dead People's house."

"Don't say that," Sarah said, leaning her elbow on the counter. "That house is the reason we can afford to rent this house. Double murder is kind of a drag on the real estate market."

Kind of? Elissa thought. Even if this mini mansion was perfect, there was still something a little creepy about living less than a mile away from a house where two people were killed. She'd asked Sarah to tell her the story three

15

times on the road trip west. Parents with a violent daughter who'd suffered some sort of brain injury. She'd woken them up in the middle of the night, then murdered them both with a hammer stolen from the tool shed. The bodies hadn't been discovered for days, and by that time no one knew what happened to the girl. They said she was fifteen, but her mental state was more like that of a small child.

"Come on," Sarah said, nudging Elissa in the side. "Let's unload the rest of the boxes."

Later that night, Elissa dumped the pasta into the strainer, letting the steam rise up in front of her. It made the hot, sticky kitchen seem even hotter. Sweat beaded on her brow. When the spaghetti had cooled, she used the tongs to carefully set a serving on each plate, making sure to keep it in the center as her dad had once instructed her. Then she added a heaping ladle of sauce and a sprig of parsley.

On the simple white plate it looked perfect—exactly the way you'd see it in a magazine. She remembered the night she'd cooked with her father, how he'd showed her these little tricks, pretending their apartment was some high-end restaurant they'd never be able to afford. He'd called the spaghetti "delectable" as if it were caviar, lobster tail, or filet mignon. He'd even faked a French accent, which always made her laugh.

She spun around, gently setting one plate down in front of Sarah, and the other right across from her. It was just seven o'clock, but Sarah had traded her jeans and sweaty T-shirt for her worn pink pajamas. Her wavy blond hair was pulled back into a bun, making her look like she could've been a senior at Elissa's high school. She held a Zippo lighter, flicking it open, then closed, letting the flame appear and disappear.

"Thanks for cooking," Sarah said, setting the lighter aside.

Elissa slid into her seat. "You can thank Dad. He taught me how to make this."

Sarah rolled her eyes. "No kidding? The whole boil-the-water, throw-in-the-spaghetti, open-the-jar thing? Wow. What a great dad."

Elissa tightened her fist around her fork, feeling like she might stab it into the smooth tabletop. Why did Sarah always have to do this? It was impossible for Elissa to talk about her father without Sarah getting tense, adding some snarky comment, or rolling her eyes. Elissa was the one who didn't have a father anymore. Elissa was the one who hadn't heard from him in over a year, who didn't even get a phone call on her birthday. He'd left because he could not stop fighting with Sarah. Everything between them was an argument. If anyone had a right to be angry, it was Elissa.

She looked down, blinking back tears. Wasn't there a

17

statute of limitations on how long you could cry about your estranged father? She'd promised herself she wouldn't let this consume her the way it had in the months after he left.

Elissa twirled spaghetti around her fork, feeling less hungry than she had just a few minutes before. Her eyes settled on the silver Zippo. It had been a fixture in her home for as long as she could remember. Back when her parents were still together, when the fighting wasn't yet intolerable, they'd sit on the window ledge and smoke cigarettes—just one before they went to bed. While it was a gross habit and they finally quit, it was something they did together. Sarah still brought it wherever she went.

"It's not like you carry that lighter around because you miss smoking," Elissa muttered. Maybe Sarah wasn't willing to admit it—but she hadn't let go of him either.

Sarah sighed. She turned the lighter over, studying it. "There are things I miss, sure. But when we were married, he was always on the road, and when he wasn't, we were always fighting. You saw it. It's better this way. Now he gets to write songs about me, and I get you."

Elissa pushed the spaghetti around on the plate. She'd heard the songs too, though she'd never tell Sarah she spent several hours a weeks on her father's band's website. "Blue Eyes," "She Said, He Said," "Back There"—those were three of the songs. She'd listened to their lyrics, waiting for there to be some hint of him coming back, of him

18

regretting what he'd done. But in the end, it always felt like the songs were about shedding excess, letting go, embracing the freedom that comes with loss.

Neither of them spoke for a long while. Sarah swallowed down a few forkfuls of pasta before looking back up. "Liss… this place," she said, glancing around the house. "This is new. This could be good for us."

"It's going to take me a while to get used to having you around."

"Come on, I gave you the biggest room," Sarah joked. "How hard can it be?"

At that, Elissa smiled. She wanted to believe her mom. Sarah had promised her that after her night shifts at the hospital they'd make dinner together, they'd watch old movies, or spend time on the back porch, working through Sarah's old record collection. She promised Elissa a whole week of Joni Mitchell, where they'd go through all her albums, Sarah playing her favorite songs as they downed Arnold Palmers in the late summer air. But part of Elissa was always waiting for things to return to the way they were—the edgy silence that always settled between them. How could a new town really change that?

Sarah stood, clearing the dishes from the table. Elissa moved to help, but Sarah shook her head. "You cooked, I'll clear," she insisted. "Go finish unpacking."

Elissa glanced up the stairs, where a stack of cardboard boxes still awaited her. She could unpack tomorrow. The sun was still hovering in the sky. There were only thirty more minutes left before it went down, maybe less. Now that she finally had a backyard…she wanted to use it.

"I just want to look around first," Elissa said. She slid open the back door and started down the steps, toward a path that wound up into the trees. She kept her eyes on rocks and twigs, careful not to trip as she kept going, moving farther up the hill, into the higher land of the state park.

The sun was lower in the sky. The abandoned house was a few yards below, a broken swing set visible from up high. She kept going, pushing beyond more trees, trying to get a vantage point to see how far back the park went. This was her new home now. Everything was going to be different—at least that was what Sarah hoped. They'd never spoken about it, but Elissa knew that beyond what had happened with her father, part of the reason they were here was because of Luca. Elissa had met him the winter before, and within fifteen minutes they were skipping seventh period to smoke a joint in his faded gray pickup truck. They'd been in school together since fifth grade, but Elissa still remembered the day she first noticed him—or noticed him noticing her.

He sat beside her in study hall, carving something into the desk with a Swiss army knife hidden in his palm. He dug into the wood, the tiny shavings falling down around his feet. When he was done he uncovered it, curving his palm so only she could see. *This blows,* it read. *Wanna get high?*

Luca was the kind of guy all the girls at Rossmore High School wanted to know, if only to say that they did. He was undeniably attractive, with toned biceps and dirty blond hair that fell into his green eyes. He always wore gray T-shirts and ripped jeans, sometimes also throwing on a wrinkled button-down on better days. He did things— smoked pot, drank, skipped class, had sex—and everyone knew it. Being around him propelled you out of whatever boring sphere you occupied and into his world, where everything was more exciting, more dangerous.

Elissa pushed through the woods, remembering the feel of Luca's hands on her skin, how he held the sides of her face as he kissed her hard on the mouth. She'd curl up in his lap, letting his hands get lost in her hair. After three months, she'd come home one night to find Sarah, red-eyed and exhausted, sitting up at the kitchen table. *We're moving,* she'd announced, without offering any discussion. They'd fought until two thirty that morning, with Sarah saying that they needed a new start, that Rossmore wasn't for them anymore. Didn't Elissa want to live in a bigger house? Go to a better public school? Moving would increase her chances of getting into a good college.

Elissa knew her mother could see it happening—how

Elissa could so easily become her: pregnant at seventeen, married at nineteen, with a daughter who looked more like a sister. She wanted to say it wasn't possible, that things with Luca were never serious, but she was afraid of something she'd suspected all along—that Sarah and her father hadn't been serious either. That part of those first years, when they were so young and when her mother had gotten pregnant, had been a mistake.

She agreed then. She didn't want to repeat her mother's mistakes.

The sky grew darker. Elissa looked back, suddenly realizing how fast she'd been walking. She was far out into the woods, and all the trees looked the same. The birds were quiet. She heard a twig snap somewhere behind her and spun around, staring into the darkness. The hair on her arms bristled. She scanned the horizon, looking for signs of which way she'd come from, when she saw her mother in the kitchen window, so far below. She turned and ran, sprinting as fast as she could, not knowing what exactly had frightened her.

CHAPTER

2

"Bombs away!" a tan girl in a purple bikini screamed. She ran over the brick patio and leapt into the pool. A giant wave surged out around her, rippling the water's crystal surface. The Reynoldses' house was three times the size of Elissa's, complete with a pool, waterfall, and hot tub. These people had money. A few guys and girls lounged around the kidney-shaped pool sunbathing, while others played Marco Polo in the shallow end.

Bonnie Reynolds dragged Elissa away from her mom, insisting Elissa just *had* to meet her son. "That's Tyler," she said, pointing to a muscular boy with electric green swimming trunks. "You should get him to show you around. Tyler's captain of the swim team, and he's just a junior. He and his friends started an after-school club for famine relief and raised over a thousand dollars last year." She raked her manicured fingernails through her highlighted hair. "Was it Africa or Tibet? Don't know, but I'm pretty sure it was one of those starving places."

Elissa nodded, trying to focus on the cheeseburgers sizzling on the grill or the inflatable pool ball that flew over the picnic table. She'd been in Bonnie's presence all of three minutes, and she couldn't stand her any longer. You could tell Mrs. Reynolds was the type of parent who thought whatever Tyler did (tying his shoes, making his bed, blowing his nose) was worthy of a standing ovation. Elissa was about to break free when Tyler—the man, the myth, the legend himself—strode over. He narrowed his gray eyes at his mom, and she sauntered back toward the adults.

"Sorry about that," he said coolly. "She give you the full treatment?" He patted himself down with a towel, flicking back a few strands of wet hair.

"Don't sweat it—moms can be like that." Elissa smiled, thankful that Tyler was at least semi-normal. "I'm sure you're really a total loser."

Tyler laughed—a real, genuine laugh, and led her over to the buffet table. There were plates of coleslaw and French fries, a tray of hot dogs, and her mom's rancid-looking potato salad. Sarah had decided to put pickles in it, despite Elissa's warning against it.

Tyler passed her a plastic plate and they both loaded up,

settling down beside some of the adults. Bonnie looked up from her small heap of salad. "So how are you settling in?" she asked, her eyes glancing from Sarah to Elissa.

"Have you met Ryan Jacobsen yet?" Tyler asked. His mother glared at him, but he ignored it.

"Not yet..." Elissa said, a little confused. She recognized the last name—the Jacobsens were the couple who'd been killed in the house. But she hadn't heard anything about a relative living in town. "Is he coming today?"

"Here?" Bonnie sputtered, her voice rising three octaves.

Ben Reynolds, Bonnie's husband, smoothed back his thin brown hair. "Gee, honey," he joked, "Did you forget to get that invite out in time?"

The entire table erupted in laughter. A couple sitting next to Sarah nearly spit chunks of hamburger onto the patio. "Oh, stop it!" Bonnie said, waving him off with a smile. She turned to Sarah and Elissa. "Ryan Jacobsen is the son of the couple who were murdered. He still lives in the house, but he pretty much keeps to himself."

"Somebody should burn that house down," a woman with oversize sunglasses said.

"Stop it, Jenny," Bonnie hissed.

The woman just shrugged. "I didn't say Ryan Jacobsen had to be in it. But come on! Why is the kid still living there?"

Ben Reynolds shook his head. "He's driving down all the home values. The town tried to buy the house. We

27

would've torn it down and donated the land to the state park."

Elissa glanced sideways at Sarah. What was that supposed to mean? Were they also considered undesirable tenants? The single mother with her daughter. The rusted Ford Bronco that sat out front. Sarah rested her hand on Elissa's leg, sensing she might say something. "It does seem a little strange that he'd want to stay in the house," Sarah tried, joining the conversation.

The woman pulled off her sunglasses, revealing heavily made-up eyes. "The house where his parents were murdered. Maybe he's crazier than his sister."

Elissa straightened up, having a hard time listening to this. Who were these people to judge Ryan Jacobsen—to judge *her*? "I can think of crazier things than living in the house you grew up in. What exactly happened?"

The table fell silent. Tyler set down his fork. "The daughter, Carrie Anne, killed her parents."

"That part I know," Elissa said, trying not to roll her eyes. "But where was Ryan?"

"He didn't live there. He lived with an aunt upstate." Tyler swiped his sun-bleached hair off his forehead.

"What happened to Carrie Anne after they were killed?" Elissa asked. She pushed back her plate, suddenly losing her appetite.

Mr. Reynolds met her eyes. "There was a massive search for her. She drowned near the dam."

"But they never found her body," Tyler jumped in. "Some people think she still lives in the woods."

Bonnie stood, dropping her plate in the trash. "Ignore him. That's just an urban legend that he and his friends believe."

"There's no way she could survive out there in the woods," Jenny said, wiping her massive sunglasses on the edge of her pink polo shirt. The rhinestones on the sides glinted in the sun.

Ben shook his head. "She had an accident outside—fell from the swings and never recovered. The girl was out of control. She'd have these horrible screaming fits. You could hear her all the way over here."

"Why wasn't she in the hospital?" Elissa asked.

"They were supposedly homeschooling her," Ben Reynolds explained. Bonnie gestured to a maid standing by the back door, signaling for her to pick up the empty plates and glasses.

Jenny let out a low, sarcastic laugh. "Right. They basically kept her tied to the radiator."

"Enough," Bonnie said, an edge in her voice. "Can we please change the subject?"

The table slowly broke into different conversations, some talking about the basketball game the night before, others speculating on when they'd finish the new restaurant at the end of main street. Elissa watched her mom push the remnants of her burger around her plate. There were so many questions about what happened in that house and what happened to that girl. But Elissa kept turning over the same ones: who was Ryan Jacobsen and how could he stand to stay there, day and night, alone?

The sun was setting when they started back down the road. They could hear the sounds of the party receding behind them. Sarah clutched the empty bowl to her chest. "So, did that freak you out a little?" she finally asked, turning to Elissa.

"Definitely—our neighbors suck. 'Maybe we should burn his house down'?" She mimed quote signs in the air. "Real nice. I wonder where they keep their torches and pitchforks...."

Sarah went silent. Elissa knew it was impossible for her to deny it. Maybe the houses in this neighborhood were classy, but the residents were not. She couldn't imagine what they were saying about them right now—this new single mother and her daughter renting the house down the road. They'd be horrified if they knew Sarah was a lowly X-ray technician at a hospital. If you didn't have an MD, PhD, DDS, or Esq after your name, you might as well be dead.

"Tyler seems pretty cool, though," Sarah ventured.

"Jury's still out on that one."

They kept walking, starting up the long driveway toward

their house. The woods were dark. As Sarah climbed the front steps, Elissa paused on the lawn, looking out beyond the trees. "Do you really think someone could live out there?" she asked.

Sarah turned back, her gaze following Elissa's. "No," she said softly. "I don't." Then she turned into the house, flicking on the light in the foyer.

Elissa just stood there, staring into the darkness. She had the strange feeling that someone was watching her. She had felt it this morning as well, when she brought the cushions out onto the back porch, arranging them on the chairs. She kept her eyes locked on a specific tree, studying a shadow behind it. She blinked, wondering if it was a trick of the light. She turned back toward the house, but the edgy feeling still followed her long after she was inside, the door closed and locked.

CHAPTER

3

Elissa got out of Tyler's car, staring up at the mansion in front of them. She hadn't wanted to come here. She'd phoned Sarah after school to finalize their plans—the first real quality time they'd spend together in... well, she couldn't remember when. They were supposed to make Elissa's signature Old Bay popcorn tonight (which tasted awesome but made your breath smell) and watch black-and-white movies on TCM. Sarah had called to bail a half hour before. Something about having to work the night shift at the hospital, being new, and not being able to say no. Part of it enraged Elissa, the fact that they'd come all this way to be the same people they were in Chicago. What was the point of Sarah spending so much time training as an X-ray technician if she was going to have the same hours as at her old bartending jobs?

Tyler bounded up the front steps and into the house, signaling for Elissa to follow. The famine relief fund-raising meeting. What fun. He'd invited her here after finding her alone on the school quad. It had been that kind of day—alone in study hall, doodling on her notebook, alone in gym, standing in the outfield for softball practice. Alone at her locker, walking through the halls, alone, alone, alone. The thought of going home to an empty house was the only thing that brought her here. That, and she couldn't help but admit that Tyler was just the tiniest bit attractive (in that traditional, he-could've-been-picked-out-of-a-catalog way).

She pushed herself forward, following him into Caitlin Aberdeen's wide kitchen. A few kids were playing video games in the living room, while a few others were drinking a pink concoction out of plastic cups. The smell of pot wafted in the air. "This is your famine relief meeting?" Elissa asked, raising one eyebrow at him.

"Hell, yeah," Tyler said, high-fiving a guy with bloodshot eyes. "Last year we gave twelve hundred dollars to a charity. It just came straight off my dad's credit card instead of us having to beg people for change in the supermarket parking lot. We can party, no hassles, and put it down as community service on our college apps."

Elissa turned away, not sure whether to be disgusted

or impressed. "I guess it does require a certain smarmy brilliance..." she allowed, staring at the crowd of kids. Maybe Tyler's morals were lax, maybe he was like every other entitled rich kid she'd known, but this was still way better than sitting alone in her house, wondering if there was some deranged murderer prowling through the back woods.

"Thank you," Tyler said, bowing slightly. He poured some vodka and pink lemonade into a cup and pressed it into her hands. "Time to get our drink on."

Elissa's head was light from the drinks. She jammed her thumbs into the video controller, steering the car away from Tyler's, but it crashed into the metal guardrail. She looked around, noticing that the party crowd had slowly devolved into various pairings. A blond girl with a low-cut top was making out with some stoner in the corner. Another couple was sitting on the back porch. She stood quickly, dropping the controller into the couch. "I believe I lost again," she said, taking in Tyler's red eyes, and the way he was half slumped on the arm of the couch. "Bathroom break."

She started up the stairs, holding the railing for support. When she got to the bathroom a redhead was hunched over the toilet, retching. "Sorry," the girl said. She'd spilled a drink down the front of her tight blue T-shirt.

"Are you okay? Do you need a ride home?" Elissa crouched down beside her.

"I just want to rest," the girl said, curling up on the thick bath mat. She wiped the sides of her mouth.

Elissa studied the girl, trying to decipher just how drunk she was. She looked in better shape than most of the kids at the party, and whatever she had drunk had already gone into the toilet. Elissa turned the girl's head to the side and folded a towel beneath it as a pillow, trying to make her as comfortable as possible. She'd check on her in twenty minutes, after she found another bathroom.

She ducked back into the hall, moving past several doors, wondering how many bedrooms one house needed. Wasn't Caitlin an only child? She started into the master bedroom, searching for another bathroom, when someone grabbed her from behind.

"Hey!" she protested, and then she saw Tyler's face.

"Tyler, you're wasted." Elissa twisted, breaking free for a moment, but then he pulled her toward the bed. He tossed her down on the king-size mattress before he tripped, falling over the edge of the bed and onto the floor.

"So? Where's your humanitarian spirit?" He stood and lunged for her, pinning her down. He grabbed her right breast with his hand, squeezing it hard. "Ahhhh...there it is." He laughed.

Elissa turned quickly, elbowing him hard in the face. She

pushed him off, running toward the door. She couldn't get her cell phone out fast enough. "Awww...calling Mommy?" she heard Tyler whine. He was up, chasing her down the hall.

"Yeah, I'm gonna need a ride, jerk," she yelled. He reached over her shoulder, yanking the phone from her grasp. They were perched at the edge of the stairs. A few people looked up from the living room, trying to see what was happening. "Give me my phone, Tyler!"

He held his hand high in the air, teasing her. There was a sick smirk on his face and she realized then that she hated him. Whatever first impressions she'd had of him—that he was a little bit of a goody-goody, that he was entitled, that he was a snob—were so much better than what she thought of him now. She'd never been so repulsed by someone in her entire life.

She pushed him hard, knocking him into the wall. Then she jumped up, yanking the cell phone away from him. It was in that moment that her arm flew back, swiping an antique lamp behind her. She turned just in time to see it fall over, smashing into a hundred pieces as it fell down the stairs.

Tyler lunged at her again. She kneed him hard in the crotch until he doubled over in pain. A crowd had gathered at the bottom of the stairs, watching. Caitlin, a short girl with an obvious nose job, pushed through some kids, noticing the broken lamp.

"My dad's going to kill me," she screeched, picking up one of the larger teal pieces. "Who did this?"

Tyler pointed at Elissa. "I'm sorry," Elissa started. "He was—"

"Get out of my house!" Caitlin yelled. The crowd fell back, some laughing. "Now!"

Elissa gritted her teeth. She pushed past them, grabbing her backpack from behind the couch. "No problem," she said, narrowing her eyes at Caitlin. "I could use some fresh air." She slammed the door behind her as she started across Caitlin's massive front lawn.

CHAPTER

4

Dammit, Elissa thought. *The point of moving here was to get away from this crap.* Outside, the road was pitch-black. She could barely see beyond the trees. She pulled out her cell phone, scrolling through her list of contacts. Every single name was someone from her old school, her old group of friends, her old life. Her mother was still stuck at the hospital. Her house was miles away, and not a single person inside the one she'd left was sober enough to drive her home—not that she would've resorted to begging. She started up the road, moving in the direction of her street. The first droplets of rain hit her bare shoulders.

She hadn't walked more than thirty feet when a car flew past, a thin spray of mud covering her legs. She scrolled back through her contacts, hovering over Sarah's name, wondering if she should try her. Hadn't her mom said to call her whenever she was in trouble? Didn't this count as trouble, standing on this unlit road, a strange car just up ahead?

The car stopped several yards away. More rain fell, soaking Elissa's tank top. The reverse lights came on as the old teal sedan sped backward, screeching to a halt. The passenger window rolled down and the driver leaned over. It took Elissa a moment to realize he was just a little older than her, with short, dirty blond hair and dark brown eyes. "Do you a need a ride?" he asked.

Elissa turned, taking a few steps back toward the house. Wasn't this the equivalent of hitchhiking? She couldn't just get in some car with a stranger. "No, this is my driveway," she called over her shoulder, trying to sound convincing.

"No, it's not," the boy called through the open widow. "You just moved in on Sycamore Lane. I live next door."

Elissa glanced back at the car, taking in the guy's flannel shirt, the stack of books in the passenger seat, and the golden stubble on his chin, as if he hadn't shaved in two days. He looked so...*normal*. "You're Ryan Jacobsen?" she asked.

The boy put the car into park. He ran his hand over his forehead, trying to hide a smile. "I'm sorry...." He half laughed. "I didn't mean to scare you. What's your name?"

Elissa looked down at her cell, unsure whether to press send. Her mother could be there within twenty minutes.

Out of all people, wasn't this boy—who lived in the same house where his parents were murdered—the last person she should be getting a ride from? "I'm Elissa," she said. "I'm cool walking, though—thanks."

She started back out, and the car rolled alongside her. Ryan laughed. "You're ten miles away from home. Let me give you a ride."

Elissa glanced at the long, winding road ahead. Just then there was a loud, rippling crack of thunder, and the rain came down much harder then before. Within seconds she was completely drenched. She glanced into the car, where Ryan was still waiting. His head was tilted to one side, as if to say, *Really? You REALLY want to walk?*

She clenched her fists together, annoyed at Sarah for having to work tonight, at Tyler for groping her, at Caitlin for throwing her out of the party. Now she was here, standing in the pouring rain, trying to decide whether or not to take a ride from an orphaned loner. Without thinking, she pulled open the door and slid inside, pushing the books out of the way.

They drove in silence for the first minute or two, the windshield wipers providing the only soundtrack. The old car was actually pretty cool, with wide leather seats and a deep dashboard. A few cassettes were stacked up on the seat, as if it were still 1989. A thin gold locket hung from the rearview mirror, and there was a yellow lunchbox on the floor by her feet.

He had a few Hemingway novels beside him, half spilling out of a knapsack, along with a massive biology textbook. She studied him, his small brown eyes and chiseled features. He couldn't have been older than twenty-one. As she watched him he kept his eyes on the road, not saying anything. Had the Reynoldses been right? Was there something wrong with him? How could he stand to live in that run-down house alone, knowing his parents were murdered there?

The silence was unbearable. The windshield wipers squeaked; the rain came down sideways, pummeling the car. After a few minutes, Elissa couldn't take it any longer. "So why do you still live in that house?"

Ryan let out a long breath, and Elissa immediately felt guilty. "I guess I shouldn't have said that," she tried, hoping they could erase the last minute, just pretend it had never happened.

"You just said what you were thinking," Ryan offered. "That's all anybody can think about when they're around me anyway. My family sent me away when I was seven, and at first that house was all I had left of them. But actually living there has been too hard. I've decided to fix it up and then sell it."

Elissa ran her fingers over the seat, pushing them down into the leather. Why did she have to go there? One minute they were driving in perfect silence, the next they were talking about how his parents sent him away. Still, it made her feel the slightest bit better than he didn't enjoy living there. He wasn't the strange loner the Reynoldses painted him as, lurking about, sleeping in the bed where his father was bludgeoned to death.

Ryan turned to her and smiled. "I heard you singing this morning. It was nice. Are you in a band or something?"

She let out a breath, relieved they were back on track. Her looked different—kinder, sweeter—when he smiled. "Yeah, I played guitar a lot back in Chicago," she explained. "My dad is in a band too, though I hardly ever see him. He's always on tour." She rifled through the cassettes in the center console, seeing if he had anything worthwhile.

"Man, these are old." She laughed, looking at the worn labels, some from the 1980s. "You gotta get some new music."

Ryan smiled. "This car was my dad's. Those were his." He looked at her for a long beat, noticing her the way Luca had all those months before. His eyes ran over her lips, her soaking wet tank top, the curly blond tendrils that were now stuck to her wet cheeks.

"So, are you and your mom here in Woodshire to stay?" he finally asked.

She looked away, noticing the Magic Eight Ball key chain dangling from the ignition. She reached for it, her hand just inches from his leg. She turned it over and smiled. "All signs point to yes."

Ryan laughed, and for the first time she wondered if

there was something more to him, this boy who everyone described as a loner. He kept glancing sideways at her, then back at the road, until the car rolled to a stop in her driveway. They sat there for a minute before either of them spoke.

"It's so quiet here," Elissa said, rolling down the window to get some fresh air. The rain had finally stopped. Ryan cut the headlights and they sat alone in the dark. "Not like where I used to live."

"It's even quieter at dawn," Ryan said. He adjusted himself in his seat, moving just the slightest bit closer to her.

"What are you doing up that early?"

"I sit out back, and I just write. Mostly stories. It feels easier. I like that time of day, because everyone is still asleep, it's like all the best thoughts haven't been taken yet." He turned to her, his dark eyes meeting hers. "Do you know what I mean?"

She watched as he studied her, his eyes falling for a moment to her collarbone, then to her tank, the wet fabric clinging to her skin. "Life's good when the rest of the world sleeps," she said. She looked down, noticing that their fingers were just a few inches apart. "Thanks for the ride, Ryan."

"You're welcome," he said softly, handing over her back-pack. Elissa strode across the front lawn, feeling lighter than she had all day. Everything that had happened at Caitlin's house seemed less painful now. Ryan Jacobsen was normal, nice…even a little sexy. Had she imagined it, the way he studied her, as though she were something to be devoured? He'd looked at her with those brown eyes, leaning in, their faces just a foot apart.

As she started up the steps, she turned back one last time. Ryan was still there, still leaning across the seat, watching her bound into the house. *No*, she thought, a smile curling her lips. *I definitely didn't imagine it.*

Inside, the house was quiet. Elissa set her bag down and moved into the kitchen to search the fridge for something edible. The shelves were mostly empty. There was still some leftover spaghetti, a jar of pickles, American cheese slices, and some unidentifiable cold cuts—salami? Roast beef? She wasn't sure. She pulled the cheese out, rolling it up the way she used to when she was a kid. Even with some food in her, she still felt off. Her stomach was unsettled. She had a slight headache—a reminder of the party, the pink lemonade–vodka concoction, and what had happened with Tyler.

Tyler. It made her sick, thinking of his hands on her, how he'd tried to pin her down on the bed. He'd been so sure that she wanted him, that he was making her night by forcing himself on her. How many other girls had he done that to? And had she been one of the few to fight back?

She glanced at the clock: 9:53. In less than twelve hours

she would be back at school, alone, trying to make small talk with the goth girl who sat next to her in English. If today had been hard, tomorrow would be worse. Now she had to watch out for Caitlin get-out-of-my-house Aberdeen, or Tyler's group of stoner friends. She thought of the crowd that had stood by the bottom of the stairs, laughing as she fought Tyler for her phone. She could still feel their eyes on her.

She was thinking about Tyler, about everything, when her mom came down the stairs. The sound of Sarah's footsteps startled her. "I didn't know you were home," Elissa said. "I didn't see your car outside."

Sarah came up beside her, resting her hand on Elissa's back. She was still in her work scrubs. "Best thing about the new house—the garage. I'm sorry, I didn't mean to scare you."

"No...I'm fine," Elissa said, feeling anything but. Whatever momentary excitement she'd felt about meeting Ryan had vanished, giving over to a sense of dread.

"Did Tyler's mom drop you off? I wanted to say hi." Sarah peeled a piece of cheese from the pile and took a bite.

"No...." Elissa looked away, wondering for a second if she should tell Sarah what had happened. "Ryan Jacobsen gave me a ride."

Sarah straightened up, a stern expression crossing her face. "You want to tell me how you ended up getting a ride with Ryan *Jacobsen?*"

50

No—she wouldn't tell Sarah what happened. Her mom couldn't even hear the name Ryan Jacobsen without getting bent out of shape. How would she feel discovering that Tyler Reynolds, perfect, president-of-the-famine-relief-fund honors student, was a date rapist? "No one wanted to give me a ride home. I started walking, and he saw me. He gave me a ride. End of story."

Sarah crossed her arms over her chest. "And you just got into some stranger's car? At this time of night? Why didn't you call me? I could've come and got you."

"Yeah right," Elissa mumbled. When had Sarah ever picked her up before?

Elissa could see what was happening. It was in the way Sarah said "some stranger." She'd turned against Ryan Jacobsen before she'd even met him. She'd eaten up every word the Reynoldses had said, bought all their nonsense about Ryan being deranged. What did they know? Who were they to talk about family values? They were helping their son run a charity club based around getting drunk and stoned.

"So..." Sarah asked, changing the subject. Her lips curled into a small smile. "How was the meeting?"

Elissa met her mom's eyes. She wanted to tell her everything. It would be so much easier to tell her everything. But Sarah was looking so hopeful, so determined, Elissa didn't want to destroy her this-town-will-change-everything dream. At least not until she had to...

51

"Tyler's a jerk," was all she said.

"Because he works hard in school and wants to get into a good college?" Sarah looked at her, the sarcasm oozing in her voice.

Elissa wanted to scream. She'd spent the whole day alone, been assaulted by some stoned idiot, then been kicked out of a party she didn't even want to go to in the first place. And now her own mother was giving her an attitude? She couldn't take it anymore—the day needed to end. The only thing good about this night was that it was almost over.

She pushed past her mom, not bothering to look back. "Right," she said, looking away as the tears welled in her eyes. "That's it."

CHAPTER

5

During fifth period Elissa strode out onto the grassy quad, scanning the long picnic tables for somewhere to sit. There was the table of techie kids, their big headphones pulled down over their ears. A few petite girls with nearly identical curly hair sat on a row, picking at their salads. Then her eyes fell on Tyler, Caitlin, Zak, and the rest of the famine relief crew. Tyler waved her over, as if he hadn't just yesterday tried to molest her.

She glared at him, then turned the other way, finding a shady spot beneath a maple tree. She settled down in the grass and pulled out her sandwich, munching while she played games on her phone, did some light reading, sent an occasional text to a friend in Chicago so she didn't look like such a loser. She'd spent all day yesterday alone—this was nothing she couldn't handle.

She was just finishing sketching a football for a drawing game, when she noticed someone towering above her. Tyler stood, his arms crossed over his chest, his eyes focused on a spot behind her. "I wanted to make sure you were okay," he said, his voice slow. "You know, our little misunderstanding at Caitlin's."

Misunderstanding? Did he really just say that? It took all Elissa had not to knee him in the crotch again. "There wasn't a misunderstanding." She glared at him until he met her gaze. "They call it date rape. And if you come near me again, I'll go to the cops. And you can put that on your college application."

Tyler just stood there, his mouth half open, looking a little stunned. Elissa tossed her phone in her bag and stood up to push past him, unable to be in his presence even a second longer. Misunderstandings were murmured words, or not realizing someone told you to meet them at nine in the morning instead of nine at night. He had thrown her on the bed and grabbed at her. What would've happened if she hadn't pushed him away, if she'd been too drunk? What if she had frozen, too afraid to fight back? The thought infuriated her.

She kept walking and was starting across the quad when she heard her name. "Elissa, right?" the person asked.

It was the girl from Caitlin's bathroom—the one who'd

fallen asleep on the floor. She looked different with her red hair pulled back in a sleek ponytail, her crisp button-down revealing just an inch of her collarbone. "I'm Jillian," the girl said. "Thanks for yesterday."

"Anytime."

Jillian stared down the sandwich perched in her lap. "I'm not much of a drinker. I got vomit on Caitlin's bath mat, and she threw a fit."

Elissa stared at Tyler's table, a group of six kids from the party yesterday. They were all huddled together. One boy had stuck straws up his nose to get the others to laugh. "Who are these people?" Elissa asked, disgusted. "Why are you hanging out with them?"

"I'm not sure, really. I used to go out with Tyler, but he's kind of a—"

"Yeah, well, 'kind of' is the understatement of the year," Elissa said.

Jillian laughed, revealing perfect, I-had-braces-for-six-years teeth. "How has Woodshire High School been treating you? I bet you miss your friends back home."

Elissa lowered her head, thinking about Luca, or Laticia, her closest friend in Chicago. She'd texted them since she'd arrived in Woodshire, but she could already feel them pulling away. It took them longer and longer to respond. How much had they had in common though, beyond smoking pot and going to the woods behind the track to cut class? When she actually thought of it, she didn't know much about Laticia's older brothers or the charter school she'd gone to before they met. Elissa had never even told her about her dad and the fight her parents had the night he'd left.

"Sorta," Elissa tried. "You should have seen where we used to live. It wasn't like here at all."

She wanted to go on and tell Jillian about the metal detectors in the school lobby, or how there was a whole list of clothing you couldn't wear because it might signal you were in a gang. Jillian was the first person to really ask her about herself, and she had this strange desire to spill everything. But before she could say anything else, two boys came up behind them. One looked like Jillian's twin, his short red hair parted to one side.

"Elissa, this is my brother, Jake, and his best friend, Robbie."

"Heard you were in a band," Robbie said. He was shorter than Jake, with hipster glasses and tight, black skinny jeans.

"How did you hear that?" Elissa asked. Ryan Jacobsen had heard her playing her guitar one morning—was it possible someone else had too?

"Google." Robbie shrugged. "Nothing is sacred anymore. Anyway…you sing, I play drums, Jake plays bass. We have this thing coming up."

Elissa blushed, knowing he must've found her old website, one she'd created two years ago when she was determined to "get her voice out there." She'd uploaded all her original songs, half hoping her dad would discover it and call her. He never did.

Robbie dug into the front pocket of his tight jeans, prying out a green flyer that had been folded into a neat square. He passed it Elissa—the paper was still damp with sweat. She opened it anyway, surprised at the block letters on top. *BATTLE OF THE BANDS*, it read, with a graphic of a guitar. Robbie shifted in his gray low-top sneakers.

"What do you say?" Jake asked. "Want to come sing with us?"

Elissa narrowed her eyes at them. "And if you suck?" she asked, only half joking. She'd been invited to play with enough "bands" to know that the good ones were rare. And she couldn't imagine anything worse than standing on stage, trying to play music, when everyone around her was fumbling to keep up.

"We don't," Robbie said. He pulled a memory stick from his backpack and tossed it to Elissa with a new confidence. "That's a recording of us. Listen to it. If you like it, come check us out—we practice tomorrow."

Jake and Robbie took off back down the quad, leaving Elissa there to think about it. She'd never been in a band, per se, unless you counted those months before her father left. They would spend good nights in the kitchen, gathered around the table, her dad moving his fingers so quickly over the neck of his guitar she could barely recognize the chords. Elissa would strum along, and Sarah would sometimes sing with her. Now her father was known entirely separately from them, the bass player for the Constants, a small indie band that toured mostly in Europe. She wondered if Robbie had discovered that too—if that was the real reason he wanted her to join up with them.

Jillian stood, glancing over Elissa's shoulder at the flyer. "They *are* good," she said. "You should go. I'm about ready to ditch the famine relief fund anyway."

She looped an arm through Elissa's, something Elissa would normally hate. But standing there with Jillian, the idea of this band on the horizon, she felt more at ease than she had since she arrived in Woodshire. Maybe, just maybe, her mom was right—maybe this was a new beginning for them both.

CHAPTER

6

Sarah stood in her hospital scrubs, drumming her fingers against the counter as the barista fixed her coffee. She checked the time above the kiosk. It was just after three o'clock, which meant Elissa had finished last period and was heading home...presumably. For the last couple of days, Sarah hadn't been able to stop thinking about Elissa, and the look on her face when she walked in the door the other night. When Sarah asked her about her first day, she'd frozen, providing only one-word answers. This wasn't exactly new for them, but Elissa looked a little shaken... scared, even. The only thing she had said was that he had gone to the famine relief meeting, and Ryan Jacobsen had given her a ride home.

Had he done something to her? Maybe Elissa was

right—maybe the Reynoldses were just closed-minded, but it *was* strange that that boy lived in the same house where his parents were murdered. What kind of person would be okay with that? And why didn't anyone in town seem to know him? She'd seen him leaving his house in the middle of the night twice in the past week, the old sedan loud enough to wake her up.

The barista handed her the coffee, and she turned, noticing a police officer standing outside the hospital's front entrance. He couldn't have been more than a few years older than her, with dark brown eyes and short black hair that was combed perfectly into place. She couldn't help herself. Before she knew it she was outside, leaning against the wall next to him, tapping her foot five hundred times a minute, trying to figure out just how to get his attention.

"Are you nervous?" he asked, looking down at her foot. He smiled, a dimple forming in his right cheek. "I usually have that effect on ladies. I'm trying to not be so devastatingly handsome."

Sarah laughed. Was this guy flirting with her? "No, no," she tried. "I wanted to ask you something. I'm Sarah Cassidy."

"Bill Weaver." The man put out his hand for her to shake.

"My daughter is seventeen, and we just moved here. We're living in a rental on Sycamore Lane. And—"

"And you wanted to ask me if I thought it was possible

that you could have a seventeen-year-old daughter. I would have to say no."

Sarah smiled. This guy was *definitely* flirting with her. "It's about Ryan Jacobsen, actually." Bill's face grew serious as she said the boy's name, his brows knit together. "He gave Elissa a ride a couple of days ago. Which is fine, I guess, but I see him coming home late at night. I was just wondering if you knew anything about him. If he's..." She trailed off, not wanting to seem too judgmental.

"Okay?"

"Exactly," Sarah said. "Finding out your parents were murdered like that, by your own sister? It's kind of intense."

Bill leaned against the wall, wiping a thin layer of sweat from his forehead. "You'd think people might have a little sympathy. I was the one who told him and his aunt. I drove three hours upstate to tell them personally. Ryan was living with this senile lady who could barely talk. I think he took care of her, not the other way around. He ended up moving back here with her, and she died last year. The kid's had a hard life. Look, I've never had any trouble with him and no one else has as far as I know. But people sure as hell like to bitch about their property values, don't they?"

Sarah stared at a spot on the concrete, suddenly a little embarrassed. Was she just as bad as that uptight woman at the Reynolds barbecue? Elissa would be mortified if she knew Sarah was going around, asking random police officers about Ryan Jacobsen. "I guess they do...." she said.

Bill turned to her, resting his hand on the radio at his belt. "I'm sorry, I didn't mean to dump on you. I just know the town board's been trying to get him out of that house for years, and it pisses me off. He has every right to be there—that's still his home."

Sarah knew, logically, that he was right. If Ryan Jacobsen was dangerous, wouldn't that have been more obvious? For years he'd lived in that house, and all the neighbors had to complain about were the peeling shingles, or the overgrown lawn. They talked about the double murder as if he himself was implicated just by being related to Carrie Anne. He'd been a kid himself. He hadn't done anything wrong.

"Thanks, Officer," Sarah said, turning back toward the automatic doors. Her break was ending, and the doctor on call was OCD about shift changes.

"Please—call me Bill," he corrected. "I'll see you around?"

He was smiling. There was that dimple again. "Sure, *Bill*," Sarah called over her should as she entered the air-conditioned lobby. She took off down the hall, chucking the empty coffee cup in the trash. He was right—Ryan was a victim himself. Ryan had a right to live in that house, and just because he sometimes drove around at night didn't mean there was anything wrong with him. Maybe he was trying to clear his head, or couldn't stand to be alone in that house at certain hours.

She went into the elevator, her stomach dropping as it rose to the tenth floor. But as she started back to the nurses' station to check in, she couldn't shake an uneasy feeling. She remembered the bright headlights shining for a moment through her bedroom curtains. If Bill was right, if Ryan wasn't dangerous, then why did she still feel sick at the thought of Elissa in that car?

CHAPTER

7

Elissa bounded up the side stairs, careful to jump the broken slats. She rapped on the door twice, noticing Ryan through the foggy glass pane. He was hunched over his laptop. Brown grocery bags were scattered over the kitchen counter. "Hey…it's me," she said, opening the door a crack. "I made you a CD."

Ryan fiddled with the web page a moment before he turned around. He looked nervous, as if she'd caught him doing something wrong. She took a few steps closer, noticing the screen. He was looking at her old website. The first song she'd ever written—"Daylight"—was paused halfway through. "That's my page," she said, not quite believing it.

"I wanted to hear more of your music," Ryan said. "That's not weird, is it?"

"Not unless you didn't like it," Elissa said, sidling up beside him.

Ryan looked down, seeming so much shyer than he'd been before. "It was beautiful."

Elissa poked him playfully in the chest. "Right answer." She laughed. She glanced around, for the first time processing that she was inside the house—the Jacobsen house she'd heard so much about before she'd even seen it. It smelled dank and musty, cut with the scent of bleach. The couch was a strange polyester print, like something out of *That '70s Show*, and yellowed drawings were taped to the fridge in the kitchen. On the counter, by the sink, there were three loaves of bread, a stack of frozen dinners, and nearly twenty cans of soup, among other things.

"Stocking the old fallout shelter?" Elissa asked.

Ryan blushed with embarrassment. "I don't like to go into town more than I have to." Elissa noticed the thin metal bars on the windows. She'd heard murmurings at school—vandals sometimes came by Ryan's house, throwing rocks through the windows. At one point someone had literally tried to burn it to the ground. Part of her understood what that was like. Maybe their old apartment outside Chicago hadn't been targeted by vandals, but there were always robberies and shootings on her block. They had security bars too, and barbed wire coiled around the fire escape.

Elissa held up the CD. "I want to play you something."

She started into the living room, where an ancient stereo was sitting on a bookshelf. The bookshelf was filled with hardcover novels, and there were stacks of more books around it, piles of tattered paperbacks and worn copies of old plays. Elissa grabbed one off the top of a stack— "Arcadia" by Tom Stoppard.

"I see you like to read." Elissa studied him, starting to piece together what it was Ryan did in his spare time. He must be one of those guys who spent days reading, studying, content to be alone. Who could he really connect with in this town anyway? Nearly every single person had heard about the murders, had been convinced they knew exactly who Ryan was before they'd spoken two words to him. He never really had a chance.

Ryan just ran his hand through his hair, brushing a few strands off his forehead. He blushed, as if getting so much attention embarrassed him. "Let's hear it," he said, nodding to the stereo. "The CD."

Elissa fiddled with the buttons, and a low, crackly voice filled the room. She'd been obsessed with the band Continuum since her dad played her their first album. She loved the lead singer's raspy vocals and the way the piano music swelled in the background. She stood there, just inches away from Ryan, watching him take it all in.

Ryan smiled up at her. "You like it?" she asked, studying his face.

"I do," he said. He did that thing again where his eyes traced over her lips, her cheekbones, down her throat to the plunge of her V-neck T-shirt. "Very much."

She turned away, feeling the stirrings of nervousness. What was it about Ryan Jacobsen that made her so self-conscious? As Ryan stood there, listening to the next song, she glided around the room, taking in the framed photos on the wall. There was one that must've been Ryan's parents. The young couple was in wedding garb, the bride staring into the camera with brilliant blue eyes. Elissa turned back, waiting for Ryan to say something, but he was still by the bookcase, lost in thought.

She walked down a narrow hallway off the living room, where another shelf of books was. She studied some of the titles, letting the music drift in from the other room. There was a door just a few feet away. She tried the handle without thinking, imagining it was the first-floor bathroom. Instead, it was a tiny bedroom. The walls were covered in bright circles—teal, pink, and purple. The bed was still covered with a musty quilt. She took a few steps in, noticing the wooden chest of toys that sat in the corner.

Elissa heard Ryan behind her. She turned, immediately regretting what she'd done. "I'm sorry...I shouldn't have come in here."

She took a few steps, trying to get around him, but he blocked her way. "You don't have to go. I haven't been here in a long time." He was strangely calm as he moved past her, going deeper into the room. He picked a teddy bear off the bed and brushed away the dust.

Elissa pulled her blond hair into a tight ponytail, twisting it hard. Why had she opened the door in the first place? "Ryan, I'm so sorry," she tried.

Ryan looked up, meeting her gaze. "When I first got here, I kept her room exactly the same in case she came back."

"How long has it been? Four years?" Elissa asked.

"Yeah, I know." He let out a sorrowful laugh. "Stupid, huh? I even used to leave supplies for her in the woods—food, blankets, even though I knew she could never have survived out there. She would've starved to death. She never could've been out there on her own. She needed constant care. My dad wanted to put her in a home, but Mom wouldn't let him. That's why they sent me away. They had enough to deal with as it was, without me in their hair."

Elissa lowered her head, not sure if she could bring herself to ask about it. Everyone in town talked about Carrie Anne, but no one ever said what had really happened to her—what made her that way. "What happened? To your sister..."

"We were playing, and she fell and hit her head." Ryan stared down at the teddy bear. "This was the bear she played with that day. I was seven and she was five. She loved that game. She'd snatch it from me and run through the house, trying to get away. I chased her out into the

75

yard and tackled her, wrestling the bear out of her hands. We laughed for a while, and then played the same game we always played—seeing who could swing highest on the swings."

Elissa could picture the little girl clinging to the swing, her tiny legs pumping back and forth. Her blond hair blew away from her face, then forward, hiding her. Ryan was next to her, reaching for her hand, but she was always just a little out of reach, the swings not yet in sync.

"I looked up at the window," he continued. "To see if my parents were watching. They spent all of their weekends in their room, with the curtains drawn, smoke wafting from under the door. They always seemed in some far-off place—I know now they were battling an addiction. I was looking up at the window, waiting for them to see. That's when Carrie Anne fell. She tumbled off the swing, hitting the ground hard. The last thing I remember is standing above her, screaming. It seemed like a long time before they came out of the house."

Elissa let out a breath she hadn't realized she was holding. It was a horrible story.

Ryan stared down at the teddy bear, slowly remembering where he was. "When she woke up she was different. She had brain damage. She would scream all the time. Break things."

"Is that why all the window have bars on them?" Elissa asked, not entirely certain what to say.

"Yeah, she didn't understand where she was all the time, and she'd run out into the woods. They were to keep her in. They're useful now, though—stops the townies when they come down here."

They stood there in silence. Ryan still clutched the teddy bear in his hands, looking at it as if it were the first time. Elissa wanted to say something to comfort him, but everything she could think of seemed false, wrong. She wanted to say she understood, but how could she? Even the worst things she'd been through—her parents' divorce, her father leaving—were nothing like this. Instead, she reached for his hand and squeezed.

Ryan leaned into her. Then he set the teddy bear gently on the bed and led her back into the hallway. "I don't like coming to this part of this house," he said softly. He shut the door tightly behind them.

Elissa looked up at him, wanting to throw her arms around him in a hug, even if three days ago they'd been just strangers. "Then we won't," she said, pulling him back toward the living room, where the music still played. "I promise we won't."

Elissa sat next to Ryan on his bed, their fingers just inches apart. The room was too small for them. There was only a narrow twin bed and a desk, but the ceiling was peaked, with a small circular window looking out into the backyard. A framed photo hung on the wall. His parents had their arms around each other. Carrie Anne stood in front with her teddy bear, and Ryan was off to the side. He looked so serious. He was the only one who wasn't smiling.

"So that's Carrie Anne," Elissa said, studying the blond girl with brilliant blue eyes. She stood in front, her mother's hands on her shoulders. "Her eyes are so blue."

Ryan leaned in, his shoulder pressing against hers as he studied the picture. "She was the heart of the family. After the accident, things changed. My parents got worse."

"What do you mean…worse?" Elissa asked.

Ryan shook his head, as if he didn't want to talk about it. "It was just different."

"Is that when they sent you away?" Ryan looked up, and his eyes met hers. He didn't answer the question, and she didn't want to push. "I know it's not the same, but everything changed when my father left. It's like everything was split into before and after. It's hard, knowing he's touring, that he's out there without us. Sometimes I wonder if he even cares about me at all."

"He must, right?" Ryan said. "He has to."

Elissa stared straight ahead. She hadn't heard from him in over a year. She would sometimes follow his band online, keeping track of their tour stops. When she was packing up the apartment in Chicago, helping Sarah put the kitchen supplies in boxes, she thought: *Berlin. My father is in Berlin.* As the days passed she thought, *Munich, Amsterdam.* All

78

the while she wondered if he ever thought of her, or if he'd been content to keep that part of his life separate, never mentioning the daughter he'd left behind.

Elissa blinked, for a minute not registering what she was seeing. The swing set was still out back, the rusted slide sitting at a strange angle. "I'm sorry," she blurted out. "I guess a divorce is nothing compared to what you've been through. It's just...I haven't talked to anyone about this before."

Ryan smiled, resting his hand on her back. "I'm glad you told me," he said. She thought he was going to say more, but instead he stood, heading downstairs. She followed, feeling like that might be her cue to go. She felt foolish for saying it, even if Ryan had assured her it was all right. It was strange though, how he'd stood so suddenly. Why had he done that? It was as if some internal alarm had gone off, and he'd realized he'd had an appointment somewhere else.

Downstairs, the house was dark. Ryan went into the kitchen, fiddling with a few of the groceries on the counter as if she weren't there. She suddenly felt so self-conscious, not sure whether she should stay or go. She grabbed her sweatshirt from the sofa and pointed to the stereo. "Enjoy the CD," she said, taking a few tentative steps toward the door. Ryan barely turned to say good-bye. "See you tomorrow."

CHAPTER

8

When she finally left, Ryan went to the door. He hovered there, waiting on the porch, watching as she took off across the lawn. "See you tomorrow," he called after her. She turned back, and he waved, his face feeling stiff and awkward. He'd never been good at pretending.

He glanced at the clock on the wall. As soon as she was inside her house, he moved quickly, pulling a can of minestrone soup from the counter and popping it open. He dumped its contents in a bowl and slid it in the microwave, watching it spin several times before it was done heating. He tested it with his finger, making sure it wasn't too hot. Then he assembled it on a tray with a few cookies. She would like this, he knew she would. Chocolate chip were always her favorite.

He went to the edge of the kitchen, opening the basement door. He started down the long flight, keeping careful balance of the tray, not wanting to spill even a drop. When he got downstairs, he kicked back a wide throw rug, revealing a trapdoor. He set the tray down as he opened it, then he started down the metal ladder, into the secret room.

He'd built it himself, reading carpentry manuals for weeks before he started. He'd bought the lumber and dug out the earth, making sure it was deep enough that no one would hear her scream anymore. He walked to the metal door he'd purchased years before, two inches thick. Her shadow passed over the peephole. He reached up, pulling the key down from the top of the doorjamb.

Ryan took a deep breath, preparing himself as he always did. He kept the tray balanced in his left hand, away from the door, so she wouldn't knock into it. As he turned the knob he checked the peephole again. Her shadow had disappeared.

He opened it and her high-pitched wail filled the air. She was hovering in the corner, next to the small table he'd bolted to the floor. It had a baby monitor and a puzzle for her to play with when she got bored. She turned suddenly, darting toward him, her blond hair falling in her face. She reached for him, trying to claw at his eyes, and he tried his best to set the tray down as he pushed her away.

He restrained her, wrapping her in a bear hug. "Easy, Carrie Anne. Easy," he whispered. She turned her head, biting into his forearm so hard that she drew blood. He winced, trying not to let go. He couldn't let her do this. He wouldn't let her hurt them anymore. He took a few steps back, pressing himself into the mud wall to stabilize them. Then he slowly bent his knees, tightening his grip as they sat on the floor.

His voice was trembling when he finally spoke. He hated her for this—for what she'd done to his life. She would always be the burden on him, always, until he died. "Why do you do this, Carrie Anne?" he asked. "Don't I take care of you? Don't I?"

When they were both sitting, he reached for the small syringe in his back pocket. He'd been buying the sedatives online for years, ordering them from a website that sent them from somewhere in Mexico. He plunged the needle into her arm and pushed down until all the medicine was injected. It took only a few moments for her body to relax. Her shoulders slumped forward, her head lolling to one side. He brushed the hair away from her face, looking into her bright blue eyes—the same ones he'd known since he was a child.

"We have a new neighbor. And I like her, Carrie Anne. Elissa and her mom moved into the Reed house, and you are going to leave them alone. Do you understand me?"

He squeezed her tighter as he spoke, unable to control the anger in his voice. She had done this to him—it was her fault. Because of her, everything had changed.

Carrie Anne's head fell forward, and she whispered something under her breath that sounded like a yes. He helped her into her bed, leaving the dinner on the small table, right beside the monitor. Then he double-checked the room, making sure everything was in its proper place. There was a wooden porch chair settled in another corner, along with a lamp with a single exposed light bulb. He felt for the restraint around her ankle. It was still there. The leather cuff was attached to a wire string, the end of it firmly anchored to the bottom of the bed. When he was certain everything was as it should be, he closed the door behind him and went to turn the dead bolt.

His heart was still beating fast from the struggle. He noticed soup spattered along the floor, which must've spilled when she'd initially hit him. He wiped up the stray vegetables and noodles with a rag he had in his back pocket, making sure he still had the empty syringe. Then he put the key back above the door, tucking it carefully in place, and started up the ladder. He'd been so distracted by the spill, he didn't realize that he never turned the lock. It was still turned to the right, the knob loose, just waiting for Carrie Anne to open it.

CHAPTER

9

"You were in his house?" Jillian held on to her backpack straps so tightly her knuckles turned white. As they strode toward the barn, Elissa listened to the sounds of Jake's bass rise up over the wind. This would be the hardest part—she knew it. Explaining to people that Ryan Jacobsen wasn't the freak they thought he was. Shattering this image that had been building for years.

"I think he's suffering from PTSD," Elissa explained. Post-traumatic—"

"I know what it is. I watch Dr. Oz," Jillian said. She straightened her red hair, which fell down past her shoulders. "I just can't believe you went over there. You're lucky he didn't turn you into a lampshade."

"Oh, stop," Elissa said, giving Jillian a gentle nudge. She

adjusted her guitar on her back. "Everyone has this idea of him, and it's just…it's wrong. He's been isolated, and it seems like he has low self-esteem, but I think he wants to start opening up to people. I mean, he gave me a ride, didn't he? He must be lonely in that house—he must."

"Low self-esteem," Jillian muttered. "Those are the ones who do all the weird stuff. I don't think he wants help—he wants in your pants."

Elissa turned, narrowing her eyes at her friend. Why did everyone have to be so crude? This from the girl who had dated Tyler Reynolds—the girl actually at one point considered him her boyfriend. Ryan Jacobsen seemed like a saint compared to that guy. Sure, he didn't fit into the picture of what other Woodshire residents imagined themselves to be. But did that mean he was a bad person?

Jillian softened. She glanced back at the old barn, listening to the music for a moment. "Do you really like Ryan? Or are you just trying to piss off your mom?"

At that, Elissa finally laughed. Jillian had only been over once since they'd met, but apparently Elissa and Sarah's tense relationship was easy to read. Maybe it was the awkward one-word answers Elissa gave whenever her mother asked a question, even if it was just: *Do we need more milk?* "Maybe I was trying to piss her off at first," Elissa said. "But I don't know. He's hard not to like."

Jillian's expression changed. She offered Elissa a half smile. "Well, if you like him, I'll at least *try* to like him.

No promises though." Then the two of them went into the old barn, where Jake and Robbie were waiting, ready to welcome Elissa into the band.

"You rocked it!" Robbie shouted out of the Jeep's rear window, calling to Elissa as she started up her front steps. She waved as Jillian, Jake, and Robbie pulled away, leaving her alone for a moment on her porch. The afternoon had gone surprisingly well. When she'd listened to Jake and Robbie's music she'd known they were good—but she hadn't realized *how* good. They played together for hours, the rhythms blending together so naturally. Robbie riffed on some original melodies she'd written, and Jake accompanied on the bass. She'd always used her laptop, recording and rerecording over tracks, then playing along with them to create original songs. But now she had to admit it—a real, live band was so much better.

She pushed inside the foyer, setting her guitar against the wall. Immediately she knew something wasn't right. It was the light—her mom had dimmed the track bulbs down lower, so the room was filled with a soft, rosy glow. She went into the dining room, where Sarah was setting the table. She'd changed out of her work scrubs and was wearing a casual blue dress and sandals.

"Mom...?" Elissa asked. "What's going on? What happened to mac and cheese on the couch?"

Sarah picked up her glass of red wine and took a sip, her eyes meeting Elissa's. "I thought it would be nice to get to know each other."

Get to know who? Elissa thought. Then the doorbell rang. Elissa spun around, noticing Ryan through the front window. *She invited Ryan to dinner?*

Elissa darted to the door, getting there before Sarah could. "I'm so sorry," she muttered under her breath. "You don't have to—"

"It's okay," Ryan said, barely looking at her. "I wanted to come." He clasped a box of chocolate chip cookies in his hands. They were in a plastic container, and it looked like a few were missing, but still...he had tried.

Elissa spun around, narrowing her eyes at her mother. She'd never been so furious. What was this? Some sort of test? Since when did Sarah care whom she hung out with? Where had she been in Chicago, when Elissa and her friends hid in an abandoned bowling alley, doing whatever they felt like? Who was she to suddenly care?

"Come sit down, Ryan," Sarah said, taking another large swig of her wine. She pulled out a chair and gestured for him to settle in. Elissa eyed the table, where a large casserole dish sat. It looked like Sarah had dumped French onion soup and corn chips together and stuck it in the oven. Cooking had never been her strong suit.

Before Elissa could say anything else, Ryan had taken his seat, gesturing for her to join him. She watched Sarah fiddle with the casserole dish, plopping spoonfuls of unidentifiable food down on their plates. "Looks good," Ryan lied. He stuck a forkful in his mouth and swallowed.

In any other situation, Elissa would've laughed, but she was too angry at her mother right now. She had gone over to Ryan's house and asked him to come to dinner...to get to know him better? Since when did she care to get to know any of Elissa's friends? "So now that he's here," Elissa started, an edge in her voice, "do you want to pepper him with questions? Give him the third degree? What?"

Sarah sat back, glaring at her. "I didn't invite Ryan over to give him the third degree," she said. "He's our neighbor. And he's been giving you rides, and you said you were over there yesterday. I just thought I should meet him, that's all."

Elissa glanced sideways at Ryan, but he didn't say anything. "Go on," she said, watching her mother. "You know you want to ask him about his parents, his house, his aunt."

"She can," Ryan said slowly. He looked up. "What do you want to know? I lived with my aunt Iris, but she had a stroke when I was eighteen. After she was hospitalized, I came back here. Back home."

Sarah let out a long breath, relaxing back into her seat. Elissa could see she was pleased—this was what she had wanted. Information. "How do you live?" Sarah asked. "Big house like that must have bills."

"Mom, I don't believe you're doing this," Elissa spat out.

"You're being incredibly rude." She moved to stand, but Ryan set his hand down on her arm. It was the first time they'd touched, with the exception of the few seconds she'd held his hand, leading him out of Carrie Anne's bedroom.

"It's okay, really," he said. His eyes met Sarah's gaze. "My parents inherited the house and a little money. When they died, I got it all. It's not a lot, but it's enough. I go part-time to Bridgeport Community. It's not the greatest school in the world, but I'm getting my credits together to apply for premed at a university. I want be a psychiatrist."

For the first time since Ryan walked in, Sarah smiled. Apparently that answer pleased her. "That's very cool," she said.

"My mom went to a psychiatrist for a long time after she broke up with my dad." Elissa couldn't help herself. She felt the words coming out of her mouth before she could stop them. She just wanted to level the playing field. It wasn't fair for Sarah to sit there, grilling Ryan about his family, his income, his life goals, and not reveal anything about herself in return.

Sarah stared at her, as if she couldn't believe Elissa had just spoken those words out loud. The table fell into an uncomfortable silence. They pushed the food around their plates, and Sarah occasionally asked another question—about Ryan's schooling, or how he liked living in Woodshire. (He didn't.) When it was clear they weren't going to eat any more of the weird, undercooked casserole, Sarah cleared some of the plates.

As soon as she disappeared into the kitchen, Ryan leaned over, his dark eyes meeting Elissa's. "It's okay—I'm grateful to be here, really. Your mom is the first person to invite me over since it happened."

Their faces were just a few inches apart. Elissa softened, suddenly embarrassed for being such a bitch in front of him. He reached for her hand, covering it with his. They stayed like that, their fingers interlocking, until Sarah appeared in the doorway.

Ryan pulled away first. Sarah set a store-bought pie on the table, along with the cookies Ryan had brought. She'd arranged them in a circle on her favorite flowered plate. Her eyes kept moving from Ryan to Elissa, then back to Ryan. Elissa could tell she had seen them holding hands.

"I'm sorry," she finally said. "I need to say this to both of you. Elissa is just getting started in a new school. I want to her to do well—she needs to. It's a big part of the reason we moved here."

"Mom," Elissa snapped, feeling the heat rise in her cheeks. "What is your point?"

Sarah didn't look at her. Instead she focused on Ryan, waiting until he looked up. "She's only seventeen."

"I'm not a child," Elissa interrupted. "This is ridiculous. What do you think is going on, anyway? He gave me a ride. I made him a CD—why are you suddenly interested in micromanaging my life?"

"It isn't ridiculous," Sarah said, raising her voice. She didn't take her eyes off Ryan. "He is twenty-one. He understands what I'm getting at. I'm asking that you respect this rule. I don't want the two of you alone in your house or this house when I'm not here."

"You're never here," Elissa snapped. She could feel herself growing angrier. Who was Sarah to sit there, suddenly acting like the perfect parent? Who was she to pretend she hadn't checked out for the last four years?

"I'm here now." Sarah held the wineglass so tightly, it looked like it might break in her hand. "Can I trust you, Ryan?"

Ryan stared down at his hand, clearly uncomfortable. "Yes, you can. But I think I should go."

He stood, twisting his napkin in his hands. He grabbed two chocolate chip cookies before turning toward the door. "Where are you going?" Elissa asked.

"You're lucky you have a mother who cares about you," he said. "Thank you for dinner, Miss Cassidy."

"You can stay," Sarah offered. It was so halfhearted it made Elissa even angrier.

Elissa stood up to follow him, but he didn't stop for her. She wanted them to be alone again—without Sarah. Things were easier then.

"Ryan—come back," she tried. But the door fell shut behind him, leaving her and Sarah alone in silence.

"I asked him to stay," Sarah said quietly.

"No," Elissa spat back. She spun around, facing her mother. "You invited him over just so you could interrogate him and then throw him out."

Sarah stood, throwing her napkin down on the table. "Honey, I am trying to protect you."

"Now? After all these years? Now suddenly you want to be a parent?" Elissa clenched her fists together so hard they hurt. All those nights came back to her. All the times Sarah had checked out, when she'd been drinking and had fallen asleep on the couch. All the times she was out until 2 AM bartending, and Elissa would have to make her own dinner. When Elissa had gotten in trouble for cutting class, Sarah hadn't even showed up at the principal's office to get her—she'd been out at a baseball game with her boyfriend of the month. There had been a whole slew of them after Elissa's dad left, as if Sarah had put an ad out for a replacement husband.

Elissa took a deep breath, trying not to cry. It was too late for them to have a real relationship—she knew that now. Sarah hadn't been there when it mattered. And no new lectures or rules could fix that. She stormed up the stairs, turning back over her shoulder one last time, knowing she shouldn't say it. It would hurt Sarah too much. She didn't mean to say it, but the words were already coming out of her mouth.

"Just because you were some wasted slut in high school doesn't mean I am."

She watched Sarah's face change, the shock and hurt registering all at once. And with that Elissa ran into her room, slamming the door behind her.

CHAPTER

10

By the time Elissa got home from school the next day, it was nearly four o'clock. As Jillian dropped her off in the driveway she noticed Ryan. He sat on a boulder at the edge of the state park, staring off into the trees. Elissa let out a deep breath, waiting until Jillian's forest green car disappeared down the road. She hadn't spoken to her mother all morning, and she planned on keeping silent as long as humanly possible. Last night had been mortifying. Her mom had been so rude to Ryan, sitting there, chugging her red wine like it was water. If anyone came away from the dinner looking like a maniac, it was Sarah.

She strode across the grass, crossing the threshold to his property, knowing how much Sarah would hate that she was doing this. When she was a few feet away, Ryan turned, offering her a small smile. "I really, really wanted to apologize for my mom last night," Elissa said.

Ryan looked down at his hands. "It's okay," he said softly as he picked at his fingernails.

"It's not okay." Elissa climbed the rock, using the natural footholds to hoist herself up beside him. "I hope you didn't take her too seriously. It was just a classic case of parent-noia."

Ryan looked at the space between them and shook his head. "We're not supposed to be alone," he said. "Remember?"

Elissa shrugged it off. Who was her mom to tell Ryan Jacobsen what to do? They were neighbors, nothing more—he didn't owe her anything. Just then she heard the phone inside her house, the ring sounding across the lawn. The cell in her pocket buzzed. She wanted to ignore it, but knew her mom would be even more suspicious if she didn't pick up. Sarah's voice was on the other end of the line. "Hey," she said softly. "They hit me with another late shift tonight. I won't be home until eleven. You gonna be okay?"

Elissa glanced sideways at Ryan, feeling the slightest pang of guilt. "Yes, I'm fine."

"And you remember our agreement?" she pressed.

"Yes, how could I forget last night?" Elissa shot back. "I'll talk to you later." She hung up, a sick feeling in her stomach. Lying had never been the easiest thing for her, but she wasn't about the give in to Sarah's demands. Just because Sarah had messed up in high school didn't mean Elissa was going to.

When she put the phone back in her pocket Ryan was looking at her. "Again, I mention how we're not supposed to be alone."

"Trust me—if Sarah wanted to make rules for me, she should've started enforcing them five years ago. It's too late now." She pointed over her shoulder at her house. "I set the home phone to forward calls to my cell."

Ryan laughed. "That's kind of devious."

"*I'm* trying to protect *her.*"

"Right…" Ryan laughed. "Well, technically we're not actually in either house."

Elissa inched closer to him, staring into the park, trying to see what he saw. "What were you looking at before, when I came up?"

Ryan lowered his head. "I don't remember much from when I was a boy, but I remember my mom sitting here, and she'd tell me that everything has a secret. Everything. Like even that tree over there is hiding something special, if you look for it."

Elissa narrowed her eyes at him. "That tree?" she asked, pointing to the birch at the edge of the forest. It looked totally normal.

"At first I couldn't see it," he said. "Then one day I could…"

Elissa looked at the tree, trying to see what Ryan was

talking about. He turned to her, resting his fingers gently on her chin. They were so cold they startled her. He tilted her head to one side, moving it just a fraction of an inch. She relaxed into it, enjoying how close he was to her, how gently he held her face.

As the angle shifted she could just make out what he was referring to. It was just like when her dad used to show her the moon. *There's a face in it*, he'd say, trying to point out the nose and the eyes, the way the man always seemed to be looking down on the earth. *See?* She never could, until one day, shortly after he left…there it was. She looked up and it was so clear to her, like an optical illusion that has just come into focus.

"Oh my God," she said softly. "There's a face." She could see the two eyes in the pitted surface, the way the mouth was formed by a long gash in the bark.

She smiled at Ryan, turning her face so their lips were only a few inches apart. His fingers still rested lightly on her chin. "People don't notice the secrets, but they're there. All around us. Hiding. Waiting to be found."

Ryan looked down at her lips, running the pad of his thumb over the bottom one. She felt like his hands were made of fire—every place he touched made her skin feel burning hot. She let him hold his hand there, waiting until he met her eyes again. "I like the way you see things," she said. "I like the way you see me."

She felt his breath on her skin. He placed his other hand

on her cheek, stroking it, then brushed back a strand of hair. She felt them moving together, then his lips on hers, an urgency to the kiss. His hands held tightly to her cheek, his fingers pressed down into her skin. She felt suddenly awake. She pulled away playfully, and smiled.

"Come on," she laughed, hopping down off the rock. "Let's break some more rules."

Ryan looked nervous, bashful even, as he followed her. She ran into his house, not stopping until they were inside the musty living room. She pulled him to her, and their lips met again. He was more assertive this time, his hand resting on the small of her back. He stroked her chin with his other hand as he kissed her, hard, on the mouth.

They fell into the couch, and she let his hands roam over her hips, grazing her stomach. Somewhere far off she heard a banging sound. He pulled back suddenly, his face tense. "What is it?" she asked.

"Nothing," he shrugged. He stood, going to the stereo. "I'm just going to put on some music."

She smoothed down the fabric on the couch, waiting for him to come back, but he kept fiddling with the stereo. "I'm going to use the bathroom," she said. Ryan didn't turn around as she left.

Upstairs, she peered into the mirror, smoothing her eyebrows and wiping a corner of her lips. It was so nice to feel this way again, without a cloud of alcohol or pot. She felt a tingling on her lips still, and she laughed a little to herself. She wondered what it must be like for Ryan to have contact after being alone for so long. She fluffed her hair and then went back down the stairs slowly, peering into the living room as she entered, expecting to see Ryan waiting for her on the couch.

But Ryan was still by the stereo and as soon as he saw her he rushed over and grabbed her arm. "You have to leave—now," he said firmly. He looked scared or angry... she wasn't sure. Elissa was confused by the sudden turn and didn't have the presence of mind to protest as he ushered her down the narrow hallway, where a side door opened onto the lawn.

Elissa felt like she might cry. "What's the matter?" she asked. "Ryan, I'm sorry—What did I do?"

She started back into the house, but he grabbed her hand, yanking her toward the door. He unlocked it and urged her outside. "You're not supposed to be here—go home! Go now!" he barked.

She looked at him, her eyes filled with tears. He stared back for a second, expressionless. Her hurt flared into anger. She turned, running as fast as she could across the lawn, back to her house, as she heard the door slam behind her.

CHAPTER

11

While Elissa was upstairs, Ryan kept his fingers on the volume dial of the old stereo, twisting it on, trying to get the right volume. Carrie Anne was up. He could hear her downstairs, and it was possible Elissa had heard her too. He spun around, making sure Elissa had closed the door of the bathroom. That's when he saw her.

Carrie Anne had somehow gotten out of her room, and escaped the restraints that held her to the bed. She was in the kitchen, searching the drawers for a knife.

Elissa was still upstairs. He heard the toilet flush, and the door opened again. He backed up toward the kitchen, thankful when Carrie Anne moved behind the low partition wall. She was shaking, he could tell. He hadn't given her the sedatives yet today.

He could see the hurt and confusion on Elissa's face, but he had no time to explain as he shoved her outside. He couldn't let Carrie Anne hurt her. Ryan's heart was pounding in his chest as he locked the side door, making sure Carrie Anne couldn't follow Elissa out. Then he turned back to the living room, carefully moving through it, turning up the volume on the stereo to muffle her screams. Turning into the kitchen, he saw her near the counter, a long knife in her hand. She didn't look at him as she bolted for the front door, pushing out into the growing darkness.

He ran after her, afraid Elissa might see them from her front window. But Carrie Anne turned left. She circled back through the woods, pumping her arms, her blond hair swinging back and forth as she ran. He sprinted after her, trying to keep her in his sight. But as the sun set, it was harder to see in the dense shade of the trees. She moved deeper into the state park, where the land opened up to a golf course.

He watched her run toward the course. A sedan was parked near the lookout point several yards away. He knew couples sometimes went there at dusk to watch the sun set over the town. No one could see her—he couldn't let them. He didn't want to yell, for fear they'd hear him. So instead he darted through the trees, moving right as she went left, hoping he could loop around and cut her off.

He never should have let Elissa inside again. He knew Carrie Anne was dangerous, and if she escaped now, if he lost her in the woods, there was the chance she'd return for them both. He tried to push the thoughts away as he ran faster, his legs burning. When he cut across the edge of the park, he saw her—her blond hair visible from a few yards away. She was focused on the car parked on the landing. He watched her, making sure the knife was held in front of her as he ran.

Within a few steps, he had come up behind her, tightening one arm around her neck. She tried to stab him, but he grabbed her other hand and squeezed it until she released the knife. Then he brought her to the ground, laying her down on top of him. He settled into the dirt, hoping they couldn't be seen from the lookout point. But there was the sound of a car door opening. A man called out, saying something Ryan couldn't understand.

He held Carrie Anne closer, squeezing her hard. He couldn't be discovered. He couldn't let her be found. She had to be so quiet now. She couldn't let out even a single sound. They stayed like that for ten minutes, maybe more, until her body relaxed against his and she was still. He regretted not giving her the sedatives this afternoon. Why hadn't he just come inside and checked on her, if only for a few minutes?

Finally, he heard the car pull away from the lookout point. The engine faded in the distance. When the forest was completely silent, he finally let her go. She tumbled off of him, her body heavy, her arms falling at strange angles by her side. "Carrie Anne?" he asked. He brushed her hair away from her face, but her skin was a whitish blue. "Get up."

She didn't respond. He shook her by the shoulders, but she still didn't move. "Carrie Anne," he said, breathless. He was starting to shake, he was so nervous. "Please?"

Then he noticed the pink and blue marks around her neck from where he was holding her. How long had he been pressing his forearm to her throat? He'd just been trying to keep her still. He hadn't wanted anyone to discover them. He leaned down, listening for her breath, but no air came out of her nose or mouth. She was dead. After all this time, trying to keep her safe—to keep everyone safe—Carrie Anne was dead.

He pounded his fists into the ground, punching over and over until his knuckles bled. What had he done? He had killed her, he had killed his own sister. What would his parents think of him now? He started to cry, heavy choked sobs. Tears squeezed out of the corner of his eyes. What was he to do?

Every moment from their childhood came rushing back to him. The first time he'd held her, when she was just a baby. That picture still hung on the wall in his bedroom. How they'd made forts in the backyard, covering themselves with the old tarp from the garage. Then he remembered his parents' faces when they'd discovered Carrie

Anne lying on the ground by the swing set, the bloody spit that covered her lips. *You did this,* his mother had said, a low fury rising in her voice. *You did this to your sister.*

He hunched over, feeling as though everyone in his life had left him. He couldn't breathe. He couldn't think. He just kept muttering her name: *Carrie Anne, Carrie Anne, Carrie Anne.*

It was 2 AM. Ryan sat at the counter of an old coffee shop off the highway. His fingernails were still caked with dirt. He couldn't stop his hands from shaking. He couldn't eat, couldn't drink. He wasn't sure he could even hold down a sip of water.

He'd found a stretch of woods off the highway and spent an hour digging the hole, making sure it was deep enough. He carefully set her body down inside it, laying a soft blanket over her. He tucked the teddy bear beside her and then covered her with dirt. He had to stop several times when he was overcome. The sadness of it doubled him over. Every muscle was tense and aching.

He hunched over, pushing the glass of water around in front of him. The waitress behind the counter was tall and thin, a blond girl in a Penn State sweatshirt. She couldn't have been more than twenty. She kept watching him, adding to his uneasiness.

"Boy, you're really working that *Rebel Without a Cause* thing pretty hard over there," she said as she poured a cup of coffee for another customer.

Ryan didn't respond. She went to the rotating glass case, where an assortment of pies and cakes spun around under fluorescent bulbs. She pulled out a chocolate frosted cake with cookie crumbs on top of it, then cut a massive piece. "Here—on the house." She slid the plate in front of him.

"That's okay. I'm not hungry." He pushed it away.

The girl leaned forward, studying him. "You gonna turn down Mrs. Hodges' mud cake? Don't let her hear you. She'll get real offended." She glanced across the diner, where a stocky woman with huge biceps was mopping the floor.

Ryan pulled the cake back, but he couldn't take his eyes off the girl. She looked about Carrie Anne's height, with dirty blond hair that fell midway down her back. She had light brown eyes and thin, delicate hands. He felt a pull to her, but he wasn't sure why. Even as she turned away, clearing a few plates off the counter, his eyes lingered on her.

For a brief moment he felt nothing about what had happened that night. He wasn't fixated on the way his arm had pressed down on Carrie Anne's neck, or how she'd looked when she fell off of him, her brilliant blue eyes still open, watching.

CHAPTER

12

"I don't get it," Jillian said, folding her legs underneath her. "Maybe it's his PTSD."

"He basically threw me out of his house," Elissa said. "He said I needed to leave."

Jillian sucked down the last of her diet soda, making a slurping sound with the straw. "If I were you, I would blow him off for a few days. Ice him out. Nothing."

Elissa clutched the neck of her guitar in her hand and stared out the barn doors. Robbie and Jake were warming up, the melody of a song—*her song*—filling the air. "I haven't spoken to him yet. I just want to know what happened," she said. "We were having fun, I thought. But then he just freaked."

Her cell phone buzzed in her pocket. Ryan's name came up on the screen. She opened it slowly, wondering if he had somehow sensed they were talking about him. She took the call but didn't say anything.

"Elissa? It's me," he said. "I want to see you."

"What happened the other night?" Elissa stood, moving to a corner of the barn. She pressed one finger in her ear to drown out the music in the background.

"I'm sorry about that...I..." Ryan sounded strange, as if he were uncertain.

"Are you okay?" Elissa tried.

Behind her, Jake played a few notes on his bass, finishing his warm-up. "Hey—are we going to play or what?" he called to her. Robbie stood beside him, adjusting the amps.

"I need to see you," Ryan went on. "There are things I need to tell you."

Elissa glanced back, watching as Robbie walked around in a circle, strumming a few chords. A ten-minute break had turned into a thirty-minute break, and even that wasn't enough time for Elissa to tell Jillian what had happened at Ryan's house two nights ago. Jake looked like he might smash his bass on the ground if Elissa didn't get off the phone soon.

"I want to see you too," she said. "But I've gotta go now. I'm performing tonight at the Battle of the Bands at school. Why don't you come?"

There was a long pause, until Ryan finally said something that sounded like "okay." She hung up the phone, feeling a hundred things at once—relieved, elated, nervous, confused. What did he want to tell her? Did he realize how hurt she was about the other day? Why had he completely freaked out?

Jillian sidled up beside her. "I would ask who that was, but I can tell by the smile on your face."

Elissa nodded, tucking the phone back in her pocket. "He's coming tonight. He wants to see me."

She would've said more, but Robbie called out to them. "Enough boy talk. We have two hours until the show. Come on, Lissa."

She went to them, listening to Jake count down the song. But as they started to play, she was more excited about the show than ever. Not just because they were genuinely good—most likely the best band competing tonight. And not just because Sarah had (in an attempt to apologize) bought her this cool glow-in-the-dark makeup that would make her radiant under the spotlights. Ryan would be there tonight, and they'd finally talk. Whatever had happened between them the other day—the kiss, that moment on the couch—had been real. It had meant something.

She moved her fingers over the frets, losing herself in the song. When she sang the first few notes, they were clearer than they'd ever been. Tonight was going to be a good night. Elissa could feel it.

Elissa studied herself in the backstage mirrors, liking the way the iridescent paint made the light dance on her skin. She'd let her hair fall down her back in her messy, I-don't-use-a-blow-dryer waves. In her tight T-shirt and ripped jeans she looked cool, relaxed even. It was times like these she wished her father could see her. There was so much of him in everything she did—even when he wasn't there to witness it.

She stuck her thumb into the pot of makeup, ready to smear some over her eyes, when she saw a familiar face behind her. "You made it," she said, catching Ryan's eyes in the mirror. She stood, not quite certain whether to hug him or not. He seemed like a stranger to her now. His hair was messy and his shirt and jacket were disheveled, as if he hadn't changed in days.

"Yeah...I wanted to wish you luck," he said. He dropped his head to stare at the floor, avoiding her eyes.

"I'm glad you came." She reached for his hands, but Robbie pushed into the room, nearly knocking Ryan over with the door. His face was panicked.

"Dude—you have the big old car, right?" he asked. "Tyler Reynolds and his friends are trashing it."

Ryan didn't even look at Elissa as he pushed past Robbie,

running toward the parking lot. She and Robbie followed behind him. The hallway was crowded with kids waiting to be let into the auditorium. But most of them had left the line and migrated to the windows. They stared into the back parking lot. One girl laughed as Ryan ran past; another boy stood there with his hand over his mouth.

Elissa's heart stopped when they pushed out the back door. Tyler had a baseball bat out. His friends—including Zak, the stoner kid she'd seen him with at school—were all egging him on. He pulled the bat back, then swung it, smashing Ryan's windshield. Zak grabbed the bat and landed another blow into a front headlight, sending plastic and glass flying.

Ryan was running toward them, his face a deep red. As soon as the crowd of boys saw him they turned. Ryan swung at Tyler and the rest of the boys jumped on top of him, one kicking him hard in the side.

"Leave him alone!" Elissa screamed. She turned, looking for help. All of the students in the parking lot stood there frozen, watching. None of them said a word as another guy punched Ryan in the stomach. Ryan tried to stand, but Tyler pushed him down. Elissa ran forward, but a boy named Curtis grabbed her and held her arms. "Get off me!" she screamed.

Tyler looked more callous than he had the night of the party. There was a slow rage burning in his eyes. As

Ryan tried to stand, he leaned over him, taunting him. "Mommy's not around anymore to protect you, is she?"

Zak circled them. His hands were still balled into tight fists. "I think he wants to show us what he had for lunch," he spat. With that, he wheeled back, delivering a kick in Ryan's side, just below his ribs. Ryan doubled over in pain.

Tears welled in Elissa's eyes. She couldn't stand to watch anyone being abused like that. "Stop it! You're going to kill him!" she yelled. But as she screamed, Ryan finally raised his head, calmer than she'd ever seen him before. Tyler charged him, whipping his leg around to deliver a blow to Ryan's face, but Ryan caught his ankle in time. He twisted it and Tyler fell, landing hard on the concrete.

Ryan stood, towering above him. His face was streaked with blood. Tyler looked scared for the first time since the fight started. A few of his friends stepped back away from them. Ryan held on to Tyler's foot and twisted it suddenly to one side. Even from a few feet away, Elissa heard the bone snap. Tyler threw his head back in pain.

Curtis dropped her arms. She stood there, frozen, as Ryan stomped on Tyler's ankle again, the bones breaking beneath Ryan's heavy boot. Tyler's face was strange. His chest heaved. It took his friends a second to process it, but Zak stepped forward, angrier than before. "You little bitch!" he yelled at Ryan.

The crowd closed in around him, ready to attack him again. But Ryan broke free just as Zak reached for his shirt.

He sprinted across the parking lot and disappeared into the woods. Elissa looked around. There were hundreds of people outside now, even though no one did a thing. A police siren howled in the distance. Curtis knelt down by Tyler's side, trying to help him.

"He's only got one place to go," Zak yelled to the rest of the boys. "Come on."

One by one they piled into his yellow SUV. The massive car screeched out of the parking lot.

Elissa couldn't breathe. Her hands shook as she took in the scene. Ryan's father's car had a broken headlight, two broken taillights, and a smashed windshield. There was a giant dent in the passenger side door. She smelled something sharp and acidic. It took her a second to realize a few of the boys had urinated on the front hood.

She staggered forward. The pavement was covered with blood. She looked down, studying the small object beside her right shoe. It was the Magic Eight Ball—the plastic toy had broken off the key chain. A few feet away were Ryan's keys, which must've fallen from his pocket during the fight. She picked them up, turning them over in her hands. Ryan was running home. The boys were in the car, trying to beat him there. If and when they did, Ryan would be locked out. Unless she left now, trying to stop them, he wouldn't have a chance.

CHAPTER

13

Robbie let Elissa off in front of her house, too afraid to go any further. "Be safe, Lissa. Don't do anything stupid," he said before pulling away. She'd begged him for a ride. As the police pulled up to the high school, they announced the Battle of the Bands had been canceled, and officers began taking down eyewitness accounts of the fight. An ambulance had shown up. The siren blared as they raised Tyler into the cab, rushing him off to the hospital.

She watched Robbie's car disappear down the road. She waited at the end of her driveway, studying the yellow SUV that was parked in front of Ryan's house. Zak lit a roll of toilet paper on fire and threw it through a side window. He was screaming something, but Elissa couldn't make out the words from where she was standing. The other boys threw a few rocks at the front windows. Two turned over a giant terra-cotta planter in the back, breaking it. When the curtains caught fire, a glow visible from the lawn, they all piled in the giant vehicle and sped off.

She ran toward the house, clutching the keys in her hand. Ryan was nowhere in sight. She bounded up the steps, trying to open the lock as quickly as she could. The smell of burnt fabric hung in the air. Inside, the living room was quiet. The roll of toilet paper was now a ball of fire, burning on the wood floor beside the couch. The bottoms of the curtains were engulfed in flames.

She ripped them down from the metal rod and stamped the fabric, not stopping until the last of the flames had gone out, the room now filled with smoke. She grabbed the charred remains and threw them in the sink. When the water was rushing over the smoldering fabric, her heart finally slowed. She let out a deep breath, relieved that she'd made it there in time.

Ryan might've still been coming through the woods, hiding out, not wanting Tyler's friends to find him. Was it possible he'd seen the whole thing? That he was up the hill, in the state park, waiting for Elissa to leave? She looked out the window, into the blackness, but she could only make out the old swing set. The motion-sensor lights had gone on, shining down on it.

She turned, the wet curtains in her hands. She opened the trash can and was about to throw them inside when something caught her eye. Underneath a few empty soup cans was an empty box of tampons and an old, dried-out bottle of red nail polish. Beside them was a discarded box for temporary contact lenses. She was reaching down for it when her phone went off in her pocket, causing her to jump.

"Where are you?" Sarah's voice called from the other end of the line.

Elissa looked out the front window. Her house stood several yards away, quiet and dark. "I'm at home," she lied.

"You're not with Ryan?" Sarah asked.

"No."

"Elissa, they just admitted Tyler. Did you see what Ryan did to his leg?"

The motion sensors timed out and the lights went off, throwing the kitchen into darkness. "He was defending himself, Mom. About six guys jumped him."

"I want you home," Sarah's voice said again. It was as if she could sense that Elissa was lying. It didn't matter that Elissa had the calls redirected to her cell. Somehow, her mother just knew.

"I *am* home," she tried again. It was too late to admit the truth. Besides, Sarah would never trust her again if she told her she was in Ryan's house—that just the other day they'd spent the afternoon together while she was at work. "I'll see you later."

She hung up the phone, fishing through the garbage

again, turning over the box of tampons in her hand. Why would Ryan have tampons in his house? Or nail polish? Was it possible he had a girlfriend he hadn't told Elissa about? Was that what he needed to confess? She reached down again, about to dig deeper, when she noticed a thumping noise coming from somewhere below. It was faint—the thump, thump, thump—constant, as if someone were banging on a wall.

She followed the noise, tracing it to a door at the far end of the kitchen. She opened it, staring down a narrow flight of stairs to the basement. She started down them, squinting into the dark. The noise grew louder. When she reached the bottom of the stairs she turned the light on, finally seeing the dryer in the corner. She opened it and the noise slowly stopped. Ryan's sneakers were inside, along with a set of damp clothes.

She pressed her face into her hands, feeling like she was going crazy. What was it that was making her feel so uneasy? What she had said to Sarah was true—Ryan had been defending himself. If he hadn't broken Tyler's ankle, the fight might have continued. Who could've said how long it would've gone on, or what else they would've done to him?

Still…there was something in his face that had startled her. She'd never seen him like that, so angry, the rage bubbling up from deep inside him. Where was he now? And why was he keeping secrets from her? She rested her back against the dryer, staring at a spot on the floor. Her eyes came into focus and she noticed the thin sliver of light running diagonally across the rug. There was a slight dip in the fabric, as if there was something underneath it.

She knelt down, pulling the rug back. Her breaths quickened. Her heart pounded in her ears as she felt along the edge of the trapdoor, where a small rope handle was fixed to the wood. Light came up from the tiny gap where the door met the cement ledge. She listened for a few seconds before opening it.

Beneath the door was a cement hallway. A bare lightbulb was fixed to the wall, brightening the space. It couldn't have been more than twelve feet long and four feet wide. She peered into it, checking to see if anyone was there. It was completely empty.

She glanced back at the basement door, which was still closed. She couldn't hear anything upstairs. Slowly, she lowered herself into the space, using the metal ladder to step down. When she was inside, she noticed the door at the end of the hall. It was similar to the front door of their house, a small peephole in its center.

She heard something behind her and spun around, checking to make sure no one was there. She shook out her hands, trying to stop her fingers from trembling, as she settled them on the lock. Before she could overthink it, she twisted the knob, pushing the door open.

The room was empty except for some basic furnishings.

It looked like a version of Carrie Anne's room upstairs. There was a short, pink table in the corner with a baby monitor and a few toys. Puzzle pieces were scattered on the cement floor. Someone had hung a pink sheet up, giving the space some color. Everyone said they'd kept her locked up, that Carrie Anne had been isolated for years. Was this where they had put her after the accident?

Elissa started into the room, studying the stuffed animals that were gathered in the corner. The puzzle looked like it was for a young girl—a unicorn was visible on one of the stray pieces. Elissa stooped down to pick it up, when she noticed the wire bolted to one leg of the twin bed. It was pulled taut. She turned, glancing over her shoulder. All she saw was a blur as Carrie Anne charged toward her and let out a horrible scream.

CHAPTER

14

Elissa threw up her hands, trying to fend the girl off, but the attacker grabbed on to her shirt, desperately clawing at her. She pinned Elissa to the floor, her tears wetting Elissa's shirt. She kept grabbing at her, ripping at her clothes, her fists pounding against Elissa's arms.

"Carrie Anne! Stop!" a familiar voice yelled.

Within seconds Ryan yanked the girl off of her, pulling her back and away. He wrapped his arm around her neck and, for the first time, Elissa noticed that a handkerchief was tied around her jaw, gagging her. The girl kept pointing at something behind Elissa. She turned, noticing a pink sweatshirt on the bed. PENN STATE was printed across it.

A cold rush came over her. She couldn't identify what it

was exactly, but everything in her body was screaming for her to run. "Get out," Ryan yelled. He held the girl tightly to his chest. "Go back upstairs, please. I got this."

She started toward the door, and the girl thrashed wildly, kicking and punching Ryan as best she could. He pulled a little syringe from his back pocket and stuck it into her arm, and within seconds she went still. Elissa climbed the metal ladder, trying to process what she had seen. That was Carrie Anne? She had stared at her with those bright blue eyes, but there was nothing deranged or crazy in them—only fear.

"Please calm down, Carrie Anne," Elissa heard Ryan whisper behind her. "You're going to hurt yourself again." She climbed the ladder, then ran up the basement stairs. She didn't stop running until she was back in the kitchen. Her whole body was shaking from the encounter. What was he doing with Carrie Anne? Why was she locked down there, and for how long?

The kitchen was quiet, the sound of a bird far off in the distance. She glanced at her house across the way, wishing for the first time she hadn't lied to her mother. Wishing that Sarah was there now, the light in the living room on, as she settled down on the couch. Her stomach was twisting, making her feel like she could throw up at any minute. Ryan felt like a stranger to her. She turned on the faucet, listening to the sound of the water rushing down the drain.

She reached for the thin stream but paused, noticing

a small piece of plastic that clung to her forearm. She pinched it off and held it up to the window, studying it in the faint moonlight. The soft, supple dome had a blue circle on it. It was a contact lens—the tinted kind.

She spun around, looking at the drawings hanging on the refrigerator. The crayon drawing of the Jacobsen family featured Carrie Anne out front, her blond hair falling down her back. Whoever had drawn it had given her huge blue eyes, just like the ones Elissa had seen in the picture of her in Ryan's room.

She felt like she was going to be sick. She went to the trash can, pulling out the empty cartons she'd seen before. The box of contact lenses was there, just below the tampon container. She read the label on its front: *Tinted Contact Lenses—Brilliant Blue*. She turned, about to leave, when something below it caught her eye.

There was a pink leather wallet with a metallic heart on the front. She picked it up, sensing what it was before she opened it. There, inside the plastic flap, was a driver's license. The picture showed a girl with thin blond hair falling over her shoulders. The birth date said she was nineteen. REBECCA OLIVER, the name read. BLOND HAIR, BROWN EYES. Tucked beside it was a photo booth picture of her and a friend, their cheeks pressed together as they smiled for the camera.

Elissa felt numb. *Oh my God*. This girl—Rebecca—was in the basement. Ryan had been keeping her there for who knew how long, pretending she was his sister. He had kidnapped her. The dots connected in her head slowly, but her body was already turned to go when she heard the sound of heavy footsteps on the stairs. Before she could reach the door, he came up behind her, yanking the wallet from her grasp.

"Give me that," he yelled.

Elissa took a step back, trying to stay calm. She smiled a half smile, hoping he would believe she'd misunderstood—that she hadn't seen what she did. But he stalked closer, his features dark. "You have to promise not to tell anybody about Carrie Anne," he said. His voice was cold. "Promise me."

"I won't tell anyone," Elissa said. She backed toward the door. She was only a few feet away from the front porch. If she could just convince him she would keep his secret…if she could just assure him of that fact, maybe she would get out of this alive.

Elissa drew her cell phone from her pocket, flipping it open. Everything her mother had said to her in the past few days rushed through her head. She'd been able to see it so clearly—that there was something amiss about this boy who lived alone in the house where his parents were murdered. *Why was I so stubborn? I didn't listen.* The thought brought tears to her eyes. She blinked them back, trying not to appear weak.

"I have to go," she said softly, scrolling down her contact list to her mother's cell. "My mom called me."

She reached the door just as she pushed send. But before she could open it, Ryan was upon her. Her grabbed the back of her head and slammed her into the wall right beside the doorframe. She saw a flash of light, then felt a violent throbbing. Her vision blurred. As she reached for her forehead, the phone fell from her hands. A heavy, dizzy feeling set in.

The last thing she remembered was his hands underneath her arms as he pulled her backward. A thin trickle of blood came down her forehead. She watched the front door get farther and farther away, the cell phone open on the floor as he dragged her deeper into the house.

CHAPTER

15

Elissa awoke a little while later. Her head was still throbbing. The room slowly came into focus. She was back down
in the hidden room in the cellar, sitting in a wooden chair
in the corner. The blond girl—*Rebecca,* she reminded
herself—was strapped down to the bed, still unconscious.
Elissa's first instinct was to get up, to run, but when she
tried to move she noticed the restraints around her wrists.
He'd tied her arms and legs to the chair with thin plastic
twine.

She looked up, watching as Ryan paced the length of
the hall. He looked agitated. He kept biting at his fingers,
ripping small pieces of skin away from the nail.

"Why are you doing this?" she asked. She tried to keep

her voice calm. She wanted him to believe that he could let her go, that she wouldn't reveal his secret—that that was still an option.

He wiped at his bloodshot eyes and took a ragged breath. "Carrie Anne *died* that day on the swings. It was my fault. She was so small, and I grabbed her hand; I pulled her off the swing and she fell. There was this horrible crunching sound. I didn't know what had happened, but her eyes went completely cold. It was like she wasn't there anymore. She was just so little...." He crumpled against the doorframe, putting his face in his hands. He kept banging his palms against his brow, as if he were trying to get a memory out of his head.

Elissa slowly processed what he'd said, the fear building inside her. Every hair on the back of her neck was standing up straight. "If she died, then who killed your parents?"

"I can't live without her. She was my sister, and it was all my fault. They said it was my fault," he wailed.

Elissa let out a slow breath. "You can live without her. You have me now." She tried to sound sweet and inviting, hoping her voice would calm him down.

He looked at her, his eyes blurry with tears. He seemed so disoriented. "You're not Carrie Anne. I can't have you both—I don't deserve it. They were trying to punish me. You have to understand. They wanted to punish me for what I did."

Elissa tried to contain the terror she felt. She wanted to scream, to try desperately to be heard. How much longer would it be before her mother got home and realized she wasn't there? Had the call gone through? If Sarah had called her back and hadn't gotten a response, she would've tried again until Elissa picked up. It was possible she knew something was wrong.

She watched Ryan rock slowly back and forth, his hands still pounding his forehead. If Carrie Anne had died years before, then Ryan must have been the one to murder his parents—there was no one else who could have done it. That seemed plausible now. She'd never seen someone so unhinged. All that time she'd believed he was still recovering from the trauma he suffered as a child, but doing okay. She felt so stupid now, so naïve. But how could she have predicted this—that he was so wildly *not okay*?

He stood up straight suddenly. Afraid he might strike her again, she felt her back go rigid. Instead, he moved methodically, untying Rebecca's restraints. The girl's body was limp as he scooped her up and started back down the hall. "I can't have both of you," he muttered. "I'm not allowed."

"Ryan!" Elissa screamed. She pulled against the twine, but it cut into her skin, holding her down. "Ryan, where are you taking her?"

There was no reply.

$*$ $*$ $*$

He was gone for twenty minutes, maybe more. It was hard to know what was happening upstairs. She thought she heard the garage door opening or the sound of a car trunk slamming shut. She watched the small baby monitor in the corner. It had a screen that showed an interior shot of the living room. She kept her eyes on it, wondering if her mother would come to the door or if he would cut across the shot, but neither of them ever appeared on-screen.

On the wall of the room was another picture of Carrie Anne. She looked older than five. In the photo she must've been twelve, at least. Who was that girl, then? Had Ryan lied about when and how she died? The photograph was taken from the side. Carrie Anne's long blond hair fell in her eyes, half hiding her face. On a mirror on the far wall in the image she could see the tiny silhouette of his parents, the mother holding the camera taking the shot. Mrs. Jacobsen's face looked strangely distant.

Elissa kept studying the girl's profile. It felt oddly familiar. She must have been at least twelve, but the math didn't add up. Ryan had said Carrie Anne had died when she was five and he was seven. Elissa was certain of that.

She looked at the slope of the girl's nose, the strange way the hair sat on her head, slightly thicker and coarser than what you would imagine for a girl who was that age. The strangest thought came to her then. *Is it possible—?*

Ryan came back. He was calmer, his body relaxed. He went to the table and started fishing through the drawers, looking for something. "What happened, Ryan? Where is she?" Elissa tried. He ignored her, pretending she hadn't spoken at all.

He was rifling through the drawer when a small, red light flashed above the door. It blinked twice and he turned, starting back out the door.

"It wasn't your fault she died, Ryan," Elissa said, trying to engage him in conversation. "It was an accident. You were so young." If she could just keep him there, she might be able to talk him into letting her go free.

"No, it wasn't," Ryan snapped. "It was my fault. That's why they punished me."

"What do you mean they punished you?" Elissa tried.

"But then I stopped them."

"Tell me what you mean, Ryan," she tried again. "Tell me what happened to your parents. I can keep your secrets."

Suddenly a voice could be heard through the baby monitor. Elissa saw a figure standing at the front door. It was a police officer—a man about forty years old. "Ryan! Are you there?" he yelled. He pounded several times on the door.

Elissa sucked in her breath, yelling as loud as she possibly could. "Help! I'm down in the basement! Please help me!"

"Ryan Jacobsen!" The officer kept knocking. Ryan

grabbed a handkerchief from the drawer and knotted it around Elissa's head, tying the end of it in her mouth. She gagged several times as she tried to scream through the cloth. Then Ryan turned to go. He didn't look back at her as he climbed the ladder, the trapdoor falling shut behind him.

CHAPTER

16

Ryan stood at the top of the basement stairs. He straightened his shirt and made sure there were no blood smears on his clothes. This wasn't his fault. He had been punished for so long; he was just trying to make everything right. Why couldn't they all see that he was trying to make it right? He wouldn't let Officer Weaver take the girl away from him. He'd already lost Carrie Anne once. He wouldn't let it happen again.

He walked into the kitchen, taking in the silhouette just outside the door. Weaver had his hands cupped over his eyes, trying to see inside the dark kitchen. He'd come to know this man over the years. Weaver said he looked out for him. He was the one who'd come by when people were outside, throwing rocks through the upstairs windows.

Weaver claimed he cared about Ryan—he said he was there if Ryan needed someone to talk to, though they he never had.

"Ryan, I was just at the hospital," Officer Weaver said as Ryan opened the door and let him in. "I saw what you did to Tyler's leg. His parents are threatening to sue. Want to tell me what happened?"

Weaver's eyes scanned the kitchen. Ryan moved in front of the trash can, closing the lid behind him. He blocked it from Weaver's view. "All I did was fight back."

Weaver rested his hands on his belt. "Listen, I'm going to do my best to get this to blow over. But I need you to stay out of trouble."

Nothing is going to blow over, Ryan thought. It was too late now. Everything was wrong. Any chance he'd had for a normal life had disappeared long ago. Everything was punishment now, punishment for what he'd done to Carrie Anne.

Ryan leveled his eyes at the officer. "You ever get tired of playing tough guy?" he asked. This was always Weaver's routine, telling Ryan what to do, pretending like he was protecting him. He'd never protected him. No one had.

Weaver let out a long, slow breath. "I'll call you in the morning so you can give your statement. Elissa's mom is worried about her. She sent me over here because she thought Elissa was with you. Have you seen her?"

Ryan's eyes fell somewhere on the floor. He picked at his

fingers, a numbness spreading out inside of him. "I saw her earlier at the Battle of the Bands," he lied. "Isn't she there?"

"No. We thought she might be at home, but she's not there either." Weaver stared him down. Ryan hated how the officer studied him, his house, as if it were his right to be here. *Get out of my house,* Ryan thought, the rage building inside him. *This is my house—the only thing I have left.*

"I'll see you tomorrow morning," Weaver said. As he walked out, his eyes lingered for a moment on the counter. Then he stepped onto the porch, the door closing behind him.

Ryan turned, noticing the girl's wallet sitting there in plain view. Weaver had seen it—he knew he had. Ryan threw it in the trash can and went to the door, locking it. He started back toward the basement, when he heard a phone ringing—Elissa's phone. In the dimly lit kitchen he couldn't make out exactly where it was. He glanced out onto the front porch, where he saw Weaver, his cell phone pressed to his ear. He had turned back to the house when he'd heard the first ring coming from somewhere inside.

Ryan scurried along the kitchen floor, moving quickly around the middle island, trying to find it. He finally spotted it under the table, the light glowing from the plastic screen. He made a dive for it. When he had it in his hands, he managed to turn it off, but it was too late. Weaver was already at the door. He pounded hard against the glass.

"Ryan—open up!" he yelled. "I know she's in there."

153

From where Ryan was hiding he could see Weaver draw his gun. Weaver broke the pane with the butt of it, then reached inside, unlocking the dead bolt. "Ryan?" he said again, stepping back into the dark kitchen. Ryan slunk deeper into the house, hiding near the pantry.

Weaver carefully moved around the kitchen, holding his gun in front of him. Ryan watched him, his eyes moving from the officer, back to the open basement door. He wouldn't let anyone take Elissa from him. She was his now, and she would be here because Carrie Anne couldn't be. She would stay with him here and he would take care of her, make everything right. Weaver would have to understand that.

Ryan pressed himself against the pantry as Weaver moved closer to the basement door. Anger pulsed through Ryan's veins. As soon as Weaver was within striking distance, Ryan kicked him hard in the back, sending him tumbling down the basement stairs.

Ryan ran after him, watching as Weaver landed with a crack on the cold concrete floor. The man twisted in pain. The memories returned, and Ryan had to blink back tears. He kicked the gun away from them and pressed his knee down into the center of Weaver's chest. "You could have stopped all this a long time ago. But you didn't. You let them do what they did. You knew. You were there."

His hands were shaking. He rocked back and forth,

pressing his knee into Weaver's chest, and the man winced in pain. Ryan couldn't stop thinking of that day—the day Carrie Anne had died. His parents had been in their room, the smoke from the drugs drifting out of the window. Their eyes were half closed when they came outside. Weaver had been there—he had watched it all happen. Back then he spent afternoons at their house getting high when he was supposed to be on patrol. *You were there*, Ryan thought, pressing his knee into Weaver's chest even harder than before. *You saw it all.*

After Carrie Anne had died, Weaver had helped Mr. Jacobsen take the body into the woods. They wrapped her tiny body in a sheet and secured it with duct tape. Then they buried her—his five-year-old sister—in a pit. Ryan still knew the spot. It was just beyond an old elm tree that twisted to the left. There was a dense patch of wildflowers that grew there.

Ryan remembered how badly he'd shaken with fear and grief. His whole body had been trembling, and he'd been crying. But his mother had been too high to comfort him. She'd seemed catatonic as she sat next to him on the back steps. When his father and Weaver had come back, they'd put the shovel back in the garage, as if it hadn't happened at all. *I don't think you have much of a choice but to go along with this Bill*, his father had said. *No one can know what happened. No one can know he killed Carrie Anne.*

Ryan pulled the switchblade from his back pocket. He'd always kept it hidden in the kitchen and had secured it when he'd first entered the house and had heard Elissa inside. He flicked his wrist and the blade came out.

He buried it in Weaver's chest, between two of his top ribs. He felt only rage as he drove the blade in. "I protected you," Weaver said, struggling against it. He reached for his gun, but it was several feet away.

Ryan's eyes were full of tears. He couldn't contain the anger he felt for this man—the man who'd helped bury his sister, who watched for years as his parents abused him. They had wanted to punish him for what happened. No, they'd never admitted it was their fault. They'd never admitted they'd been locked away in their room getting high. It hadn't been *their* fault—they'd reminded him of that every day. It was his. "No, you protected yourself. You protected them. Even though you knew what they did to me."

He watched as Weaver strained against the blade, then went limp. Blood covered his hands. Ryan hated him—he hated him for letting them do it. He had only been seven years old. They had punished him for what had happened, and they would've kept punishing him if he hadn't stopped it himself.

When Weaver was completely still, Ryan let go of the blade, falling back on the floor. The smell of blood was in the air. He hated it—he hated them. He took a breath, trying to calm himself as he sat there. It was over—Weaver was dead. They were all dead. He had stopped them.

When he finally caught his breath, he wiped his hands on his pants, smearing them with blood. The wave of anger subsided for a moment. Then he pulled open the trapdoor, disappearing again below it.

CHAPTER

17

Ryan had been gone for several minutes. Elissa watched the officer appear and then disappear on the monitor, and now she could hear a scuffle somewhere above. She strained against the rope. She couldn't move her hands at all, only her ankles. She kicked them away from the chair's sturdy wooden legs, trying to loosen the bonds.

A metal lamp was only a few inches away. It was three feet tall, the bulb exposed. She heaved and twisted her entire body, moving the chair just a little bit forward, toward the lamp. She pushed her ankle out, reaching with her toe until she kicked the lamp forward. It wobbled a bit. She kicked it again and again, until it fell toward her.

The searing hot bulb landed on her forearm. The pain was excruciating. She winced against it, trying hard not to scream. She leaned forward, nudging the bulb a little farther down her arm until it landed on her wrist. The thin rope started to melt. The air filled with the smell of smoking plastic. She moved her wrist up and down, trying not to scream as the rope melted on her skin.

The cell door had fallen closed. She heard the trapdoor creaking open and the heavy sound of footsteps on the ladder. She moved quickly, freeing her hand, then working at the other wrist, trying to untie the other rope. It took her a minute before she was able to unknot all three restraints. The skin on her arm still burned. It was red and swollen from where the bulb had touched it.

The footsteps came closer. Elissa darted behind the door, pressing herself against the wall so he wouldn't see her when he came in. She tried to stay perfectly still, even as the rough concrete dug into her back.

Slowly, the door opened. She inched toward it, hiding against its cold metal back. Ryan stepped inside the small cell. Every muscle in her body tensed at the sight of him. There was blood all over his hands and on his jeans. He was hunched forward, his fingers gripping a knife. He took in the corners of the room—the twin bed, the chair where Elissa had been, the burnt rope. Before he could turn she darted around the door, pulling it shut behind her. She turned the lock quickly.

Ryan pounded his fists violently against it. He threw his whole weight into it, shaking the wall. She climbed the ladder as fast as she could and let the trapdoor fall flat. She took in the dank basement. It was then that she saw the officer's body. Blood pooled around his right side. His eyes were still open. Her fingers tensed in a fist.

She looked around the room, trying to find something to seal the trapdoor shut. Ryan was screaming in the cell below. Her head still ached. Now that she was standing, dizziness threatened to overtake her. She grabbed the edges of the washing machine, trying to steady herself. She took a deep breath and with a few hard pulls she managed to get it a few feet from the wall. Then she went behind it, toppling it over the trapdoor to weigh it down.

She darted up the basement stairs, feeling for the knob. She twisted it, but it didn't give. She tried it again and again but it still wouldn't open. Her heart was racing, her entire body shaking with the realization: She was completely trapped.

She went back down the stairs, feeling at the officer's waist. His gun was gone. He had handcuffs, a few bullets in a leather case, and a flashlight. She tried his pockets, but there wasn't anything useful. She took the thick metal flashlight, hoping she could use it as a weapon if she needed to.

Think, Elissa said to herself. *Think think think.* Far below, she heard the cell door bang open. Ryan was screaming as he climbed the ladder. "You better get back here," he yelled, his voice filled with fury.

The washing machine was halfway over the door, but he strained against it, the wood slats creaking as though they might break. She scanned the room, using the flashlight to figure out what was there. Besides the washer and dryer, there was a water heater and a wall of metal pipes with some old cleaning supplies and concrete blocks. In the corner she found another door. She slammed her shoulder into it, bursting into the garage.

She spun around to try and secure the door, but there was no way to bolt it shut. She darted toward the garage door, yanking up on the handle. It wouldn't budge. In the dark she could only see flashes of the room. She looked at the edges of the wall, trying to find a button for a garage opener, but there was none in sight.

She climbed into the car, and sat in the driver's seat, groping with her fingers, feeling the ignition. No keys. Nothing. The inside of the sedan, looked so different now. This was the car he'd kidnapped Rebecca in. He'd brought her here, possibly giving her a ride the same way he'd given Elissa a ride two weeks before. She tried not to think about it as she rifled through the glove compartment, looking for anything she could use as a weapon. There were only maps and a few old cassette tapes.

There was a noise behind her, and she spun around, checking the garage door. It was still closed. She noticed then there was a small glass window in it, but there were no signs of Ryan. She pulled the yellow lunchbox from the floor and opened it. Her hands started to shake. Inside was a bottle of chloroform and two thick rags. There was a bunch of the same plastic twine he'd use to tie her hands. This was what he'd used to take the girl. When was he planning on taking her? How long was he going to wait before he killed them both?

She looked up, catching a glimpse of something in the side mirror. Before she could react, Ryan sprung up, grabbing her by the throat with both his hands through the open window. She tried to scream but nothing came out. Her body writhed against him, but he fought her, his top half pushing into the front seat of the car. As she kept struggling, her nails digging into his skin, she heard the doorbell sound. It kept ringing, the person pushing it over and over again. Even as she fought him, the strength slowly leaving her body, she somehow could sense who it was.

Her mom had found her. She wasn't alone.

CHAPTER

18

Ryan managed to get the door of the car open. Elissa kicked at him, trying to keep him away, but he grabbed one of the rags and pressed it to her face. It was still damp with chloroform. Her resolve left her. She started to see black at the edges of her vision, and her body went slack. She was not able to fight him as he dragged her out of the front seat and around to the back. Her limbs were weak. With one quick motion he heaved her into the trunk, locking her inside.

It took several minutes for her to regain consciousness enough to realize where she was. She felt for the flashlight she had jammed into the back pocket of her jeans, switching it on. There, just inches away, was the girl she'd seen in the cell. She was curled into a tight little ball, her body rigid. She was dead. Elissa couldn't breathe. She turned, trying to get as far away from the body as possible.

She rested her back against the side of the trunk and began kicking as hard as she could at the place where the backseat would be. Her legs hurt from using so much force. She kicked again and again, jabbing the heels of her boots into the same spot. Slowly, the upholstery started to give. She maneuvered around and dug her fingers into it, feeling the thin carpeting that covered the back of the trunk. She yanked it back, pulling a layer away.

Then she started kicking again. The whole car rocked from the motion. *I will not die in here*, she thought, the anger swelling inside her. *I refuse to let him kill me.* She landed one final blow into the back of the seat and her leg went through, pushing down the center console. She pried at the upholstery until she created a big enough space to squeeze out of. When she was finally free of the trunk, the girl's body still locked inside, Elissa grabbed the flashlight off the front seat and felt its heft in her hand. Then she lay back for a moment and listened to herself breathe.

Sarah paced the length of the porch. She rang the doorbell again, waiting for someone to appear. The lights in Ryan's house were off. The kitchen window was broken, and it smelled like something was burning. She pressed the doorbell again and again, knowing in her gut something was wrong. Elissa wasn't at home. She wasn't at school. Sarah had called her cell six times, and it had gone to voice mail. Where was she? And where was Ryan?

She thought of the X-ray again, and her stomach twisted. The doctors couldn't believe any one person could've done so much damage to someone's ankle. They went through the eyewitness accounts, trying to piece together what had happened. They were certain he's smashed Tyler's leg with some blunt object—a pipe or bat. The bone was shattered, the break so vicious they'd been surprised Tyler hadn't passed out from the pain.

Sarah pulled out her cell, dialing Officer Weaver's number again. He'd left the hospital over an hour ago, assuring Sarah he'd find Elissa. She'd waited there, expecting him to at least call back—but nothing. Now his car was sitting here at the edge of the driveway, empty.

She rang the doorbell again. Finally, a light went on. Ryan appeared from the far end of the kitchen. He opened the front door a crack. "Hi, Mrs. Cassidy," he said calmly.

Sarah studied him. The side of his face was swollen, presumably from the fight in the parking lot. There was a small cut above his lip. But he had changed into a clean shirt and jeans. She glanced over his shoulder, but the kitchen looked organized—everything in its place. "I'm looking for Elissa," she said. "Is she here?"

"No, ma'am."

"She's not at home—I thought she was with you." Ryan

looked at his shoes, using the toe of his boot to press a loose floorboard into place. She nearly felt guilty for a moment, coming here, insisting that Elissa was in his house. He seemed so meek, so…childish.

"No…she's not here, Mrs. Cassidy," he repeated. He went to shut the door, but Sarah pressed her shoulder into the house, stopping him.

"Look, I'm not angry or anything. I just want to—" The motion-sensor porch light clicked off, throwing them into darkness. Ryan's face slowly came into view, and she noticed the glowing smears across his cheek and on the back of his hands. Shimmery, iridescent paint covered his skin. It was the glow-in-the-dark makeup she'd bought for Elissa. The same kind she'd picked out just a day before, as an apology for being so stern.

"Ryan…do you mind if I have a glass of water?" she asked. "It's been a long day for both of us, I'm sure." She pushed past him into the dark kitchen. There was no fear in her. She knew Elissa was here, inside somewhere. Her daughter needed her.

Ryan pulled a glass from an upper cabinet and filled it with water. Sarah took it from him, trying to stop the shaking in her hands. They stood there, facing each other, Ryan just a few feet from her. Sarah eyed the knives on the counter behind him. It was impossible to know if he had a gun, or if Weaver was here somewhere, being held inside the house as well.

172

Before she could say anything, she heard a faint scream coming from somewhere below. It was Elissa's voice—she would recognize it anywhere. Sarah darted to the door at the far end of the kitchen and yanked it open. But before she could get down the first step, she felt the pain rip through her stomach. A knife stuck out of her side. She fell back, landing hard on the floor, watching as Ryan's features changed.

He looked more assertive, calm even, as he tugged the switchblade out of her flesh and put it in his back pocket. Then he grabbed her ankle, yanking her down the stairs, down into the abyss.

CHAPTER 19

When Elissa got to the door between the garage and the basement, she jiggled and twisted the knob, but it wouldn't open. It must've locked from the inside. She screamed again, hoping her mother could hear her.

She felt the glass pane in the door, trying to figure out how thick it was. It was two feet wide by two feet tall—big enough for her to slip through if she could break it open. She banged on it with the metal flashlight, but it didn't even crack. Sticking the flashlight into her waistband, she scanned the garage again. This time she noticed a toolbox sitting on the far wall. She rifled through it and found one of those smaller hammers that have a ball on the front instead of a flat hammerhead.

She swung at the glass pane again and again, not

stopping until it shattered. She hit the edges, where the doorframe met the glass, making sure she had enough room to slip through. Above the doorway there was a metal pipe. She grabbed hold of it and lifted her legs up, swinging to slide down through the small window.

The back of her legs scraped against the remaining broken glass, the blood welling up to soak through her ripped jeans. She was back in the basement. The officer's body was still there. The washing machine was overturned on its side, shoved away from the trapdoor. She didn't see anyone else. *Where is my mom?* She started back for the stairs but heard something above her. Someone was coming. She shrank back, hiding behind the old water heater in the corner, the hammer still clutched in her hands.

Ryan started down the wooden steps, dragging something behind him. The body slid forward, landing at the bottom of the basement stairs with a dull thud. Elissa blinked back the tears. Her mother was lying on the cement floor, one arm outstretched, her limbs completely still. There was a wound in her side. Her shirt was ripped and covered with blood.

Elissa stayed there, watching her mother's chest, which still rose and fell with each breath. *She's alive,* Elissa thought. *You have to help her.* Ryan dragged Sarah toward the garage door, but he stopped when he noticed the

178

broken window. Elissa pressed her body against the wall. She crouched low, hoping he couldn't see her.

"I want you here with me," Ryan said, speaking to the darkness. "But I need Carrie Anne back. I need her back—I need to make it right. And if you can't do that for me, Elissa, I can't keep you."

Elissa buried her face in her hands, inching farther into the narrow space filled with pipes, concrete blocks, and old tools. She could sense there was a small room somewhere behind her. Ryan left Sarah's body and started toward Elissa, his footsteps echoing in the concrete basement.

The single lightbulb buzzed above them. Elissa heard each one of her mother's choked breaths. Ryan crept forward and, for an instant, their eyes met. He lunged at her, but Elissa jerked herself backward, through the pipes and into a small alcove where the furnace was. She struggled to stay on her feet, her eyes locked on the cop's gun, which was still sitting on the floor three feet away. She could hear Ryan right behind her. He moved past the pipes and came up behind her as she dove for the weapon, her arms burning as she slid across the concrete floor.

He snatched at her ankles, trying to drag her back to him. As she wrapped her hands around the butt of the gun, he let go of her legs. When she turned back, ready to fire at him, he had already run to the other side of the basement.

He was fiddling with a fuse box. In one swift motion he threw a lever, sending the entire room into darkness.

She squinted, waiting for her eyes to adjust. She remembered the flashlight at her belt, clicking it on. It showed only small circles of the pitch black basement—the wall with the fuse box, her mother's body, the broken garage door. She held the gun in her other hand, thinking Ryan might have escaped through the garage. Then she took a step to her right and saw him dart out from behind the water heater, the knife aimed at her throat. She fired three times, the bullets hitting him in the stomach. He staggered backward. Then he curled up against the wall, his head falling forward as he stopped moving.

Elissa went to her mother, using the flashlight to find her way. She hovered over her and pressed her fingers to her side. The stab wound was deep. It was hard to stop the bleeding. "You're okay," Sarah gasped, reaching for Elissa's face. The tears came quickly, slipping down Elissa's cheeks. "We're okay."

Elissa set the gun down and held tightly to her mother, burying her face into her neck. *I'm sorry*, she wanted to say. *You were right.* But all that came out was a low, choked sob, as her terror gave way to relief.

She was looking up the stairs, wondering if she could carry her mother out, when she remembered that the door locked itself. "We need the keys," she whispered, looking back over to Ryan's body.

"No," groaned Sarah.

"It's okay, Mom." Elissa smoothed some hair off her forehead and then moved slowly over to Ryan, fumbling around in his pockets, looking for the keys.

Suddenly, his hand shot up and grabbed her wrist.

Elissa gasped. "Ryan, please, you have to stop!"

He looked at her with such pain, such emotion, that she almost felt sorry for him again. "I can't," he said simply.

She managed to jerk her arm out of his grasp, but the force knocked her backward onto the ground. He rose up above her, bringing the knife into the air with his other hand. "It will be over soon," he said. "Just close your eyes."

"It's over *now*," rasped Sarah as she staggered to her feet behind him. She grabbed the ball-peen hammer Elissa had dropped on the floor and swung it through the air.

Ryan sagged to the ground, the knife clattering to the floor, his blood pooling around him.

It was over.

EPILOGUE

Two weeks later, Elissa loaded the last of their boxes into the back of the SUV. The day was cooler than normal, the wind coming through the trees. She and her mother were starting over...again. Going back to Chicago, to a two-bedroom apartment three blocks away from their last one. Elissa would return to her old school, to Luca and her old friends. Sarah would work at the hospital in the city. But nothing would be the same—nothing could ever be the same again. It had turned out Elissa's grandmother was wrong. A place *could* change you.

Elissa watched as Sarah locked up the house and started down the front porch. She held onto the wooden railing, taking each step one at a time. She still struggled to walk, even though the stitches had already been taken out. Elissa had promised she'd do all the driving during the two-day road trip, even though Sarah winced whenever she took left turns.

Across the lawn, the Jacobsen house was roped off with police tape. In the last weeks it had served as a constant reminder of what had happened there. Ryan, who'd survived despite his serious injuries, had been institutionalized. The house had yielded up one last terrible secret of the Jacobsen family: videotapes from the years following Carrie Anne's death, with old family movies. In them, Ryan was dressed in Carrie Anne's clothes. He was wearing a wig, and blue contact lenses. After the accident, his parents had used him as a replacement for their daughter, addressing him only by her name.

For years they'd kept him locked in her room, alternately celebrating family events with him and abusing him. Psychiatrists concluded he'd turned violent from the stress of the abuse. He eventually snapped and killed them both. Afterward, he'd gone back to his role of Ryan, the estranged brother, but he kept up his parents' charade, kidnapping girls and turning them into Carrie Anne. He'd kept them in the secret room, locked up, treating them in the same way his parents had treated him. He kept repeating the cycle, and probably would have for many more years, if Elissa and Sarah hadn't discovered his secrets.

Even now, in the institution, under the influence of strong sedatives, he still called out for his sister.

Elissa's gaze fell on the tree at the edge of the state park—the same one Ryan had showed her weeks before, as they sat on the boulder. Sarah walked up and rested her arm around Elissa's shoulder. It felt good to feel her mother there, right beside her. For once, Elissa could look at her mom without thinking about what Sarah had and hadn't done—about the past, the divorce, or the tumultuous years that had followed. Elissa now thought of Sarah only as the person who'd saved her.

"What are you looking at?" Sarah brushed a few strands of hair away from Elissa's face.

Elissa pointed to where the tree stood. She tilted her head, but the face didn't appear to her now. She wondered if it had ever been there at all, or if in Ryan's presence she had somehow imagined it. "What do you see?"

Sarah was quiet for a long time. "A tree?"

Elissa smiled, squeezing her mother's hand. "Yeah, that's what I see too."

Sarah furrowed her brows, as if she wasn't quite sure what the significance was. Elissa wanted to tell her she was sorry, that she knew how wrong she'd been. In the past days those words had never made it past her lips, though they ran on a constant loop in her head. What mattered now though, she realized, wasn't whether she said it or not. For the first time in her life, she and her mother were beginning to see things the same way. It was in everything they did—how they cooked together in the kitchen, how they settled down on the couch together every night. Elissa always picked up when Sarah called.

"Ready to go, Liss?" Sarah asked, starting back toward the car.

Elissa didn't let go of her hand. Instead, she let herself be pulled along behind her mother, their arms stretching out but still linked.

"I've never been more ready for anything in my life."

ACKNOWLEDGMENTS

Thank you to the amazing people at Relativity, FilmNation, and Poppy.